# A STIRRING IN THE NORTH FORK

## Mark Torres

# Dedication

*For my wife and children who complete me.*

# A Note From the Author

One day while driving with my wife on the Long Island Expressway, she turned to me and said "let's drive to the end." What we found was the bucolic countryside of Long Island's North Fork region with its beautiful vineyards and lovely people. Now, all these years later, we still venture out to the area as often as we can to take in its timeless charm.

# Acknowledgements

This book is dedicated to none other than my wonderful wife **Migdalia Ortiz-Torres** whose spirit, strength, love, and belief in me has made this project possible. While the so-called rules of authorship suggest that you must have lent written words to a project in order to be deemed an author, I am proud to say that my wife did everything possible, both conceptually and practically, to make this project a reality. Therefore, as we have done with our lives together, WE have created a story that we will forever be proud of, and I am eternally grateful.

I wish to thank my children Isabella, Jake, and Olivia, who inspire me every day to be the best I can be. I also would like to thank my dear mother Grace; my family and friends; Richard Hull, my friend and professor; Amy Folk for her historical assistance; Angie Mangino for her critical review; Dave Bass for his technical assistance; all of my dedicated colleagues; and all those who have touched my life, no matter how big or small, in ways that have lent creative inspiration to this book.

# 1972

It was a cool first evening of autumn. The busy summer season was winding down, and Maria Cruz looked forward to working less hours. She had been pulling double shifts for the last three months at a local motel in Greenport, New York where she worked as housekeeper. She lamented getting home far past her daughter's bedtime. Things will be better now, she thought. As she approached her car, she fumbled for the keys in her purse. This distracted her from noticing the hulking figure rushing up behind her. A sharp blow to the back of her skull rendered her immediately unconscious.

Maria awoke to an agonizing pain in the back of her head. She was unaware of how much time had passed or where she was. The taste of blood lingered on her lips. Blindfolded and face down, Maria tried to roll over but realized that her hands and legs were bound too tightly. She felt the rush of the outdoor air while being whisked away in the rear of some unidentifiable vehicle.

When the vehicle came to a halt, her abductor exited, pulled her by her feet, and tossed her onto the hard ground face first. The abrasive surface caused the blindfold to slide off, but before she could focus on his identity, he leveled three hard blows into her face, instantly breaking her nose and crushing some teeth back into her throat. Her head recoiled to the ground, nearly causing her to lose consciousness again. He then grabbed the mane of her hair, and began to drag her.

With her hands bound, Maria desperately tried to dig her nails

1

into the fertile soil in a hopeless attempt to resist her assailant from dragging his quarry further into the field. She could not believe this was happening, and was in no condition to put up much of a fight. Her bloodied nose was horribly broken, and her bruised right eye permanently shut. Her left eye was barely open enough to catch the brilliant moonlight. She tried to scream, but could only manage to whisper the word "Please," as she coughed up blood and teeth.

The unknown brute continued to drag her across the vast swath of open land somewhere in the North Fork of Long Island. Her abductor chose this location with sinister precision. The last of the summer tourists in 1972 had made their exodus weeks ago, and he knew there wouldn't be another soul for miles. Maria vaguely knew this place as well, having spent many days strolling in a nearby field picking flowers with her young daughter. Only the cruelest of fates could turn this place laden with fond memories into the scene of her tortuous nightmare. The brutal procession continued on with nary a watchful eye other than the nesting ospreys; the raptors who have long made their aeries in these parts.

When they reached what was to be her final resting place — a shallow grave that her abductor previously fashioned — the man brought down his boot to the side of her face, dislodging several more teeth and shattering her jaw. He then began to roll her help-less body in a tarp made of clear plastic, and secured her body with duct tape. Then the brute kicked her once more, this time to the left side of her chest breaking some ribs, and inched her body near the makeshift sepulcher. Still alive, but now gasping for air, Maria welcomed death as much as she feared it.

Her left eye remained fixated on the vivid moonlight radiating through the plastic. It was her only solace from the violence being inflicted upon her. So bright was the moon, she thought, until the opening of a car door interrupted her gaze and another figure approached.

"Bitch," said the person in a voice that Maria knew all too well, and as she turned her head to confirm the identity, the man brought down his knife into her chest over and over again. Maria gasped each time he drove in his blade. As the moonlight in her eyes began to fade forever, thoughts of her daughter lingered with the realization that she would grow up without a mother, and without ever knowing the evil that had befallen upon her.

Just before the blackness consumed her life, the one who was now retreating back to the car said, "Good riddance."

# Black Rhino

I had it all...or at least I thought I did. Being accepted into the New York office of Powell & Mason, the world's most prestigious law firm, with a cushy salary of $175,000 per year, had me beaming with thoughts of a lavish lifestyle. And why not? I, Savoy Graves, had toiled for many years as a blue-collar union grunt earning about a quarter of my current salary. It is September 2009. With a law degree and a great job, after paying my dues, now the sky's the limit.

Despite these visions of grandeur, I always felt a bit misplaced. This is a result of being about 10 years older than most of my new colleagues. Unlike them, my real life experience offered me a broader vision of the world. Prior to joining the firm, I was proudly working as a building engineer at an esteemed university in New York City for nearly twenty years. By all accounts, it was a noble career founded upon an attained skill in a certified trade at a well-established employer with excellent benefits. This position also included tuition reimbursement, which allowed me to attend college to earn a bachelor's degree. Serving as a shop steward for our local union provided a great opportunity for me to represent my fellow co-workers in all of their job-related matters. It was this role, the one I fancied as "the great defender" that directly led to my interest in going to law school.

There were very few area law schools that offered evening programs to students like me who needed to work in the days and attend class at night. I was warned how crazy of an idea this was, but my financial situation afforded me no other option. Being a bachelor allowed me the freedom of enduring these long hours without having to answer to anyone, but there was no escaping the incredible workload. So, acutely aware of my lot, I applied, and was accepted into, a top-notch law school in New York City. My new schedule included the grueling pace of a 40-hour workweek performing manual labor, while simultaneously enduring the intellectual demands of a four-year legal education.

A wise friend once told me,

"If you fail to plan, you plan to fail."

This could not be more relevant to my situation. Well, not really planning. No one could possibly plan for the madness of working full time while attending law school. Instead, I devised an unbreakable schedule so meticulous that it itemized reading and study times by each law subject every day for four years. Vacations from work were not to be used for leisure, as they should have been. They were used exclusively for study time and extended leave from my job was used to study for the bar exam, which to me, can only be likened to a personal and spiritual climb to the top of an intellectual Mount Everest.

Four years of law school, while working full time, raged on, and to my great satisfaction, it didn't break me. But that is not to say that it was all a fairy tale ending. To the contrary. I was clearly disadvantaged in the merciless academic shark tank that is law school. Leaving school each night to go home and rest for work the next day, while my classmates were cramped into the library studying and retaining information from the day's lesson was very frustrating. For me, study times could only be reserved for the weekends and days off from work. This naturally had an adverse impact on my grades, which directly disadvantaged the onset of my legal career.

You see, in the world of Big Law, grades were prized far more than anything else was. So I really had to step up my game. My marketability centered on a unique background of real life experience, which clearly separated me from the rest of the pack. In this world, I always thought of myself as the anomaly, like the rare black rhino. Not that I would have the audacity to liken myself to this magnificent creature that is on the precipice of extinction, but my background and life experience doubtlessly made me a rare breed in the world of Big Law which claims to desire diversity.

Still, I was no match for my colleagues, affectionately referred to as the Courtney's and the Geoffrey's, whose academic careers made them well suited for the glorified, but suffocating, offices of Big Law. Here they toiled for 80 hours a week, churning out research for the senior attorneys and partners, who take all the credit and lucrative pay for their efforts. I never begrudged my colleagues, though. They come from a life of privilege, which is certainly not a fault, and likely has its own challenges. They are great people with brilliant young minds, many of whom are destined for great things once they figured out their course in life.

I had been repeatedly warned about life in a law firm. The largest firms, which give rise to the term Big Law, send out recruiters to all the area law schools in hopes of attracting law students to work summer internships at their firms. These students are wined and dined during these internship programs while paid at the same salary as the firm's junior associates. Upon successful completion of the program, which is almost always guaranteed, these students receive an offer to join the firm as an associate after graduation with the promise of power, prestige and an exorbitant salary. However, once they join, the wining and dining ends, and these new attorneys are thrust into the pressurized setting in which they are required to reach over 2000 billable legal hours per year. With eyes wide open to the realities of the Big Law system, I trudged along, riding my wave of experience, ambition, and strong work ethic, hoping to change the world.

Nearly a year had passed with me remaining fully submersed in my work. Having access to world-class legal resources to tackle interesting problems faced by prominent clients was intoxicating.

The money, too, which was badly needed to handle my debt that had quadrupled from student loans, was so incredibly satisfying. Admittedly, the prestige of working at a world renowned law firm actually started to get to my head somewhat, but relying on my instincts, I continued to keep my head down, work hard, and always have an open mind to learn new things.

Then on one idle Tuesday morning, all junior attorneys were summoned to a meeting on the 30th floor of the firm's monolithic headquarters. Without warning, me, along with dozens of other upstart attorneys, were stunned when the director of the firm announced that many of us would be immediately laid off. The economy was still struggling from the collapse in 2008 with many of the Big Law firms continuing their dramatic downsizing. At least that's what he told us.

Denial is a funny thing. Even though the economy was in the tank, and the proverbial hatchet was being brought down on many of us, part of me thought that such a fate would somehow elude me. After all, Savoy Graves is a survivor. This couldn't be my fate. So I scurried back to my office to continue reading some old cases related to my current project when the phone rang. I was summoned to a random office and immediately told that my employment will end within two weeks. A generous severance package was being offered, along with documents for me to sign, which included a waiver preventing my employment with the firm in the future. That was it. It all ended in a blink of an eye. The prestige, the work, and most of all, the money. The former blue-collar grunt who always relied upon the job security that union members enjoy, was swept up by the greatest fear I've always had; being out of a job at the worst possible time in my life.

# Reverie

Hand in hand, the two ten-year-old girls ran blissfully in the field. Their target was the red and green swing-set in a park overlooking the East River in New York City.

"I call green," said Lola.

Angie, running slightly ahead of her, staked her claim to the red swing. The pair swung for an eternity in the warm spring day.

Lola's Grandmother Lita sat on the bench with Angie's mother chatting the afternoon away. After their swing, Lola and Angie played a quick game of tag before settling onto the great lawn overlooking the water.

"Isn't this so much fun?" asked Angie.

"Sure thing, chicken wing," replied Lola.

"Lola, tomorrow is Parents' Day in school," said Angie, as Lola sighed at the thought of attending such an event without ever having parents. "Are you coming to school?"

"We'll see," said Lola, who then tapped her friend's shoulder saying, "you're it" before running off.

Her childhood reverie was interrupted by a family friend seeking to pay respects to Lola for her loss. Lola offered a brief smile and a deep hug for the mourner. They both stood before Lita, dressed in her favorite blue dress, as she lay peacefully in a coffin adorned with flowers and pictures.

"She was a great woman," said the lady.

"She sure was," replied Lola, "She was my mother and father all rolled up into one."

The woman slowly moved on as Lola retreated back into her seat.

For her whole life, Lola Cruz had been raised by Lita. The name Lita is short for Abeulita, which in Spanish means Grandmother. Lola had always been told that she was born somewhere in Long Island and, after the sudden death of her mother, was relocated to New York City when she was still an infant to be raised by Lita. For her entire life, Lita was the closest semblance to parents that Lola would ever know. Now, at the young age of 22, Lola stood mourning the loss of her beloved Lita whose life was cut short by a massive stroke. Several mourners paid their respects, and after saying the final prayers, Lola made her way to the apartment, where for the first time in her life, she will live alone.

The next morning was overcast, with rain expected. It always seems to rain during funerals, Lola lamented, as she prepared for the burial. She wore a simple black dress. Her hair was up; her pain was visible. The final resting place of her beloved Grandmother is in a simple plot in a cemetery in Queens, New York. Long ago, a distant relative managed to secure this location for her burial. Without such family support, there would have been no money to pay for a final resting place for her body. Lola met the few loved ones she had in front of the nearby church, and together they travelled to the cemetery.

Lita was to be buried at the far corner of the cemetery adjacent to a large green wrought iron fence. Across the street was the entrance to the elevated train station that overlooked the cemetery. As the trains roared above them, Lola wondered what the passersby would think as they looked down. Would they recall the sad memory of a loved one or remain indifferent as they went about their commute? The rain, which held out until the services finished, now began to fall steadily. Most of the mourners had left and, except for one elderly woman and a few cemetery workers, Lola was alone. There was another service nearby that Lola watched from a distance. She could see a young girl dressed in a purple dress holding what appeared to be the hands of her parents. Lola wondered whose hands she would hold now. Such thoughts have haunted her whole life.

The pain of growing up without ever knowing either of her parents has left a permanent hole in her Lola's heart. She has long dubbed this hole as the *"void"*, and throughout life, on most occasions, particularly those involving family, it would always remind her of what she had missed. Lita doubtlessly did her best to fill the void, but that chasm was too vast to bridge, and now that Lita is gone, she doesn't even have that. As Lola watched this little girl clutching the hands of her parents, she half smiled at the girl's blessing, although it is blessing she would never get to realize.

# Nothing Spared

I returned home in complete despair and began to sob. This was a deep sob, not quite out of self-sympathy, but more out of desperation. My career had been derailed at such an early juncture and my debt was an immutable force staring me dead in the eyes.

Grief shifted to anger as questions rattled in my brain. Why was I let go? Was it my age? Not bright enough? Did my self-proclaimed "anomaly" status wear off? Surely, there must be some form of discrimination or other foul play involved. That is when I lost it. In a fit of rage, everything within reach was thrown at the wall. The TV remote control and a dirty glass from the night before were my first targets. My rage migrated into the office area of my apartment where the books on the built-in bookshelf became the next target. Books, pictures, office supplies, papers; nothing was spared. I stood above the vanquished pile of debris in the middle of the floor, almost in some perverse admiration.

The nearby liquor cabinet offered a measure of relief. Although never known for being much of a drinker, I popped open a bottle of whiskey and began to gulp it down. The initial sting of the whiskey in my throat made me cough. Yet, after a few seconds, the drink had a soothing effect. With my rage now quelled, my focus returned to the debris strewn across the floor. Seated next to the pile the combination of the fatigue from my wide ranging emotions and the whiskey, caused me to pass out. The phone rang, perhaps from a concerned neighbor who may have heard my rant, but I had no intention of answering any calls. My life was on hold.

My sleep was interrupted by the licks on my face from my dog Clubber. Tilting the scale at nearly 100 pounds, my golden retriever was a great dog, not just for the obvious undying devotion and playful banter exhibited by all golden retrievers, but just as much, for the way he always knew when to stay out of my way during difficult times. And this was a difficult time.

Clubber came home with me after a visit to a pet store in Canarsie, Brooklyn several years ago. When I arrived at the store looking for a prized "show dog," he was in a pen with his larger sister. Vying for my attention, she kept bullying him out of the way, but that only caused me to push her aside and her younger brother leapt into my arms. There was no mistake; he was the one. I always had the heart to stick up for the little guy, and he was no exception. My grandiose ideas of Clubber starring in dog shows across the country never materialized, but he was a true companion in the purest sense. And there he was, trying to revive his old buddy, after witnessing my fit of rage and its not so pretty aftermath. With a nudge, the type that he is all too familiar with, Clubber trotted away allowing me to fall back asleep.

The next morning brought no change to my self-doubt, with the fears from my financial pressures still mounting. The hardwood floor of my study looked like a war zone, and my faithful companion patiently waited for me to match his motivation. Aside from quick trips to the bathroom, and letting Clubber into the courtyard adjoining my apartment to do his business, this would be my place of solace to contemplate my situation. It was just me, Clubber, and a bottle of whiskey, which upon finishing sent me into another deep slumber. My sleep was interrupted by a warm sensation on my head.

"Clubber, get away," I snapped.

But the sensation persisted, and my eyes opened to see the dog snoring on the sofa across the room. It must have been a drunken stupor. Still, the warm sensation on my head was inexplicable. It seemed like a gentle hand. Whatever it was, comfort was not on the menu for me, but anger and despair were, so I brushed it away. Then, the warm touch stroked my head again. Clubber, who was perched on the sofa, let out a yawn and stretched his legs before barreling over to me. I hoped to ignore him, but he would have none of it as he let out a thunderous bark and picked up his leash to demand a walk, and he would not be denied.

# Force

Luther Vale never thought of himself as a racist. In his mind, doing so would dignify the existence of anyone who is non-white and therefore deserving of rights, and he'll be damned before he is ever accused of subscribing to that notion. While he was not born with his extremist views, they were certainly something he embraced with full vigor. His father, Erik Vale was a hard man. By day, he worked diligently to provide for his family. By night, he was a drunk, a bad drunk, who regularly beat his wife Hanna and their only child. Despite his shortcomings, Erik Vale was a prominent figure in the North Fork, and the reach of his power in the area was long.

Forever fearful of disappointing his father, Luther excelled in school, and eventually applied for a career in law enforcement. At 20, he joined the Southold Police Force and quickly made his way up the ranks to detective, and by the time he turned 23, he became a lead detective on the force. There was no mistake to everyone, but Luther, that his meteoric rise on the force was due to this father's power. This naturally inflated his already narcissistic personality. When both his parents died in a car accident several years later, Luther vowed to carry on the family's proud legacy. To do so, he formed his own company, one that provides private security to several of the affluent families in the North Fork region. Luther felt that providing a valuable service to those in power automatically transmuted that same power to him. After all, power and prestige is what Luther craved the most.

Luther's narcissism and racial bigotry are equally matched by his misogyny. Not that he didn't love a woman's physical attributes. In fact, he enjoyed women of all kinds, sizes, and shapes. This was true regardless of their race, creed, or color. After all, in Luther's eyes, women were only good for one thing: pussy.

While he has dated several women, some of whom he would categorize as a serious relationship, Luther's views would inevitably become exposed to his partners, who always sought to retreat from the relationship, giving way to the familiar feelings of rejection, which he abhorred. Luther Vale was never formally charged with domestic abuse, but that certainly doesn't mean that he never engaged in threatening behavior and violence, particularly against women.

"It's only illegal if you get caught" was a favorite motto of his. Standing at six feet four inches and over 250 pounds, Luther was a formidable physical force, and he made a living by "putting a hurt" on people.

On this evening, Luther was brimming with anticipation as he waited for her to get out of work. He had watched her for some time. Sure, she was Spanish, but, hell "I would tap that ass anyway" he reasoned, and judging by her former lover, she must have some fine pussy. He had seen her many times before in that tight little maid's outfit. He often wanted to sneak up behind her, bend her over, and give it to her as only a strong white man can do. But he would never dare to touch her at that time for fear of jeopardizing his position. So he bided his time until things blew over. Now, almost a year later, he would make his move. He would apply his forceful charm and finally take what he wants, what he deserves.

The woman exited the motel, stopping to talk with a coworker. Her wavy hair was drawn up in a bun. He liked that look. It would give him the ultimate power to pull it free while taking her from behind. In the light, he could see a glistening shine off her full lips. Moist, no doubt, from being licked by her sensuous tongue, he thought. Now touching himself, Luther admired her curves with excitement. Her full hips were ripe for breeding, although he would never dream of breeding such filth. He would use her solely for his pleasure, and leave her to spasm from multiple orgasms, satisfied that a real man took her the way she needed to be taken.

The woman parted ways with her coworker and approached her powder blue 1960 Chevy Nova. The ten-year-old car was a beat up shit-box, thought Luther, who fancied himself to be an automobile aficionado.

As she drew closer, Luther exited his car, approached the woman, and said "Hello Maria."

Maria was surprised by his appearance, but smiled nonetheless. "Hello Mr. Vale. What are you doing here?"

"I was just passing by," Luther said slyly. "What say you and I go to the diner for a bite to eat?"

Blushing, Maria politely declined his invitation, and reached for her car door. Luther obstructed her path, leaned on the door, and grabbed her waist firmly. Maria tried to pull away, but he pulled her closer to him, grabbing her buttocks as she could feel his erection press against her.

"Luther, what are you doing?"

Smiling, Luther responded, "Come on, Maria. I know you've always wanted me. You were too busy with that little sissy boy you were fucking, and we both know that you need a real man."

Without warning, Maria let loose a hard slap to his face, drawing a speck of blood to his lower lip, causing him to ease his grip slightly.

Luther wiped his lip and smiled. Wrongfully calculating her reaction as some form of aggressive foreplay, he was pleased at the thought of her liking it rough. He pulled Maria in again, this time even tighter. With a force she had not realized she possessed, she raised her knee right up into his testicles. Luther yelped, released his grip, and stumbled to one knee writhing in pain. Maria tried to enter her car, but the hulk continued to block her path. She instead turned to go back to the motel, but he grabbed her arm again preventing her from leaving.

The lust in his eyes had been replaced with raging anger as he said "You spic cunt. You're going to turn me down?"

The look in his eyes made it clear that he would not relent, so with one of her keys clutched between her index and middle finger, Maria swung at Luther catching him in his cheek leaving a four-inch gash. His recoil forced him to release her arm and she fled back to the motel. Wiping his face, he stood in disbelief that this woman, who was beneath him in every possible way, had the nerve to reject him.

"That bitch," he uttered as he stepped into his car and sped off.

# Resolute

We returned from our walk, which took longer than anticipated. A quick shower helped me relax before getting into bed. It's been just over 24 hours since my employment was terminated and the urge to start planning my next course of action was growing. The rest of the evening was spent researching vacant attorney positions on my laptop until falling asleep. The next morning, my job search resumed. There were a few leads, so I began applying for various positions. One position that stood out clearly from the others was an associate position at a small firm specializing in labor and employment law. Even though it paid half my previous salary, it seemed like a place to gain a great amount of experience. I was fortunate enough to be able to schedule an interview for the day after next.

After an early breakfast, I entered the lobby of the Brooks & Cane Law Firm. To the right of the entrance there was a library stacked with aged law books. A small conference room was set across from the library and a hallway led to several offices in the rear. A middle-aged receptionist with a raspy voice took my name and asked me to have a seat. The rough lines on her face showed the signs of someone who has worked too hard, and her voice was of someone who's smoked cigarettes for far too long. A few moments later, a short plump gray haired man in an old suit came to greet me. He introduced himself as Roddy Brooks and he led me to his office.

Mr. Brooks' office was a like a makeshift museum of all things related to unions and the Labor Movement. Old banners and slogans from the many labor related actions he had been involved in were strewn about in no particular order. Signs like *"Strike now"* or *"I'll give up my union card when you pry it from my cold dead hand"* adorned the floor of his office, along with many scattered papers and books. He quickly shuffled a full ashtray into the top drawer of his desk, as if the strong smell of smoke permeating in the office would not give away his rampant smoking habit. He caught my eyes as I spotted one of the posters.

"Yes," he said, "that was my first encounter on a strike line. It was supposed to last just two weeks. Instead, it lasted almost two years! Those sons of bitches gave us hell, but they eventually caved."

He broke his moment of nostalgia and said, "So, you are interested in joining our firm. Tell me a bit about yourself."

"Well," I replied, "I have extensive experience as a union employee and a shop steward of a union. I put myself through college and eventually law school. After graduation, I landed an associate position at Powell & Mason and worked there for some time before being laid off."

"Sorry to hear that," said Mr. Brooks. "Those bloated Big Law pigs got too big for their britches. Employers throw a ton of money at those firms to keep unions out."

Mr. Brooks spent the next half hour detailing the history of his firm, the work they do, and spoke of the glorified legacy of the Labor Movement. His passion was captivating and the camaraderie made me feel that this firm would be a good fit for me. Then, Mr. Brooks paused and said that the firm has other candidates to interview before making a decision on the position.

"As you may know, there are a lot of attorneys looking for work," he said. "We'll get back to you when we have made our decision."

"I hope to hear from you soon," I said as we shook hands and parted ways.

My commute home was filled with the thoughts of the friendly, albeit unproductive interview, which did nothing to alter my jobless state. Even though that position paid far less than my former position, it would be a good fit for me. It was the type of job where I could put my very expensive legal education to good use in helping hard working union members. But until they've completed the interviews, there was nothing to do but wait.

Legal positions in this economy were at a premium. Many attorneys and other professionals with higher degrees had changed careers altogether. Some junior attorneys even resorted to flipping burgers in fast food restaurants just to make ends meet. Yes, it was that bad. Not only was my lifelong student loan debt hanging over my head, but, so too, was the possibility of being thwarted from the very reason I went to law school in the first place: to help people. There had to be something, but nothing appeared on the horizon.

Lost in deep thought, I nearly missed my train stop. I have lived in Sunnyside, New York for over a dozen years. The many local taverns, restaurants, and diverse population in this small part of Queens, just minutes from New York City, makes this a great place to live. Exiting the train station, I stopped off at a local bar to ponder my next move. The Front Pages Grille has been a fixture here for years. It's a true local dive that only regulars could call home. It boasted a beat up pool table, a tattered dartboard that has seen many a match, and an old style jukebox, whose limited songs include *"Take Me Home Tonight"* by Eddie Money, and Billy Idol's cover of the Tommy James & The Shondells hit, *"Mony Mony."*

I sat at the bar and began to consider other career options. A return to my former career as an engineer crossed my mind, but there was no guarantee of being rehired, and even if I did, it wouldn't pay enough to cover my student loans. I've always been an excellent writer, but had no experience as an author of non-legal work, and from what I've heard, the publishing industry is ruthless. Nothing was clicking.

Depressed, I left the bar and walked for what seemed like an eternity. It was a warm spring night, the type of weather that has always invigorated my spirits. But even the anticipation of spring could not alter my mood. There was no escaping the fact that both personally and professionally, I was in big trouble.

There is a quote I've read that warns against staring at the abyss for too long lest it shall begin to stare back at you. With that in mind, I was determined to reverse my self-absorbed calamity, and welcomed the next day with the hope of new prospects. A hot cup of coffee jumpstarted my internet search in a job market already saturated with brilliant and out-of-work attorneys. Even now, swimming hopelessly with the Courtney's and the Geoffrey's proved to be my lot.

Several hours of a fruitless job search, forced me to recoup and clean up a bit. My self-made war zone of an apartment had to be straightened out. The books were replaced on the shelves, the broken glass was swept up, and my best tape job on the remote control did the trick. This simple household chore made me feel productive, and it felt good. Wanting to build on that feeling, I gathered my laundry and headed down to the laundry room.

My cooperative apartment is on the first floor of a six story pre-war building. There weren't too many tenants, but just enough to make vying for the three washing machines a serious competition. I've had some mean races with some of the elderly women in my building who, if left unattended for longer than a few seconds, would not hesitate to remove my clothes from the machines and dump them onto the nearby table in the laundry room. Today, I had enough laundry to occupy all three machines, and to my pleasant surprise, all three were available.

After loading the machines, I studied the library in the laundry room. The so-called library was really just a collection of old dusty books that have been donated over the years by the building's occupants and stored on a rickety bookshelf. Among the reading collection was a series of old newspapers neatly bound within plastic covering to ensure their preservation. I gently pulled down the newspaper collection and scanned through the catalogue. To my astonishment, the collection was very well organized and well preserved. It contained a wide array of newspaper articles, in sequence by date, from the 1960's to December of last year. The collection had articles varying from large publications like the *Washington Post* and the *New York Times* to more local rags like the *Queens Herald* and the *Times Newsweekly*.

I sat down at the table and began to delve into the collection. I've always been fascinated by stories of the past and this catalogue didn't disappoint. The political coverage of the time was intriguing. So, too, were the random sports stories. Even the vintage department store advertisements, with their antiquated designs and obscenely low prices compared to today, were amusing. The loud buzz from the machines, indicating the completion of the first wash cycle, did little to interrupt my reading.

My catalogue search paused at a random newspaper called the *Long Island Sound*. I was careful to unfold the delicate parchment, which was dated Friday, October 21, 1972. The headlines were dominated by the contradictory stories of both the Vietnam War and the proposed peace talks.

Then I saw a small article towards the bottom of the third page with the headline:

**"Woman found dead near an open field on Long Island".**

The story continued.

*"The body of a woman, identified as Maria Cruz, aged 22, of Puerto Rican descent, was discovered earlier this month in a shallow grave in a field in Orient, New York. The bludgeoned body was wrapped in plastic with multiple stab wounds to her chest. There are currently no witnesses to the gruesome crime."*

A victim of a jealous lover immediately came to mind as my curiosity grew.

The article continued: 'Detective Luther Vale of the Southold

Police Force added; *'We currently have no witnesses and are asking all North Fork residents who may have information to please contact the Southold Police Department.'''* The wash cycle for all three machines was now complete and I rose to place the wet clothes into the jumbo dryers quickly before returning to the table..

The story of a murdered woman in the early 1970's in eastern Long Island neatly tucked in the middle of some obscure newspaper would not ordinarily garner much attention. After all, bad things happen all the time. But there was something about this story that intrigued me. Yet, there was nothing further to the article and there was no other mention of it in any of the other publications. This irked me.

In my youth, my Grandfather would prop me on his lap and together we would read the newspaper each night after dinner. We would discuss the stories in earnest for hours. Building on my interests, my Grandfather would pick out one specific article each week and ask me to follow up on the story. Over time, he learned that crimes and mysteries intrigued me the most. Many of my days as a youth were spent searching for the slightest bit of information to report back to my Grandfather. He would affectionately call me his "little detective" and I loved it.

This story reminded me of those times and my interest in researching this case grew by the minute. After all, since being laid off, I've had an insatiable longing to sink my teeth into something, and this seemed like as good a thing as any. I snapped a picture of the article with my cell phone, and replaced it along with the remainder of the catalogue back to its proper location. After the buzzer to the dryers went off, I gathered my clothes and went back to my apartment.

Along with a solid legal education from a reputable law school, I've always possessed a naturally keen mind with a staunch attention to detail, traits that began in my youth as the "little detective." Once latching onto a project, there was no letting up until my search reaches a conclusion. Up to about a half an hour ago, the death of Maria Cruz was completely unknown to me. But now, fully gripped by the case, and a longing for a meaningful purpose, I was determined to find out more.

An initial internet search on the murder yielded no results. That was not too surprising. After all, this case was found in a completely random manner among a rare collection of newspaper articles in my laundry room. Still, my frustration grew over the inability to find anything more on this story. I expanded my search to more general terms, but that mostly yielded travel information or other commercial activity about the recreational activities, vineyards, and lodging in the area. Information on the newspaper that ran the story, the *Long Island Sound*, was also futile because that agency is no longer in operation.

It seemed that a more hands-on approach would be required, so I researched the local libraries in the area and found that the largest is located in Riverhead, New York. After placing a call to that library, I was delighted to learn that they maintain a large newspaper archival collection, including articles from the *Long Island Sound*, dating back to the early 1900's, which is accessible for viewing on their microfilm machines.

A plan was finally in motion and the Riverhead Public Library would be my first stop. For now, this would be my new job, and why not? The job market wasn't expected to yield any real options in the short term and the severance package I received from Powell & Mason could hold me down financially, for a little while at least. Since time was going to pass by anyway, I may as well be engrossed in this fascinating story. Hell, at the very least, a few days off enjoying the beautiful countryside of the North Fork of Long Island could serve as a much-needed distraction from my jobless state.

# Lion's Head

Comfortably nestled between both the South and North Forks of Long Island lies Shelter Island. At roughly 8,000 acres, this island is the home to many affluent families and is a popular destination for visitors. To most, the island is only accessible by ferry to and from Greenport for the North Fork, and North Haven for the South Fork residents. To the wealthy, it is also accessible by yacht or small seaplanes. The island boasts several restaurants, hotels, and bed & breakfasts. One third of the island is comprised of the Mashomack Preserve, an area established by a nature conservancy to preserve the island's variety of plants and animals bordering 10 miles of coastline.

The Rivington family has made Shelter Island their home for well over a century. The estate is perched on a ridge overlooking the magnificent Gardiner's Bays and the Shelter Island Sound. At nearly ten acres, the property has an adjoining cottage with its own private beach, an Olympic sized pool, and a nearby dock that can host at least one large yacht. The grounds are perfectly manicured with giant hedges and a waterfall fountain. The front of the house is guarded by tall majestic iron gates adorned with a lion's head crest and the family name beneath it.

John Rivington and his wife Eleanor lived at the home with their two children, Winston and Ethel, the latter of which died at the young age of 10, leaving Winston as the sole heir. Never fully recovering from the death of her daughter, Eleanor Rivington struggled with depression her entire life until her death in 1949.

The family patriarch John Rivington died two years later leaving the entire Rivington fortune to the well-educated, and very wealthy, bachelor heir. Winston then met Sarah Forsythe on Shelter Island, and, after a brief courtship, the two got married at a grand wedding held at the estate.

Winston and Sarah had two children, Charles and Rosemary, who were born and raised on Shelter Island without having a want in this world. Charles Rivington, who is widely known as Chet, is the older of the two siblings. He is handsome, athletic, and rich, which made him a natural target for the many women hoping to marry into such staggering wealth. Chet wasn't naïve though. He knew the game, and played it well.

At 16, Chet lost his virginity to not one, but two, beautiful female escorts; professionals brought in for the occasion. Since then, Chet has developed the wide reputation as a philanderer, a playboy who enjoys using women at his complete discretion. Just 14 months younger, Rosemary was blessed with beautiful facial features and cursed with a frigid demeanor. Many suitors have tried, but failed, to survive her overbearing personality. Rosemary was reputed to be prim and proper in their world of high society, which really meant that everyone knew to fear her.

Chet and Rosemary enjoyed the finest lives that money can buy. For them, the most difficult of choices was to decide which private schools and country clubs to attend, and what part of the world they should visit next. Such a life, however, is replete with its faults. In this society, the pressure of living up to the family name and legacy is eternal, and the guardians of such a staunchly protected lifestyle were the Rivington parents. They instilled in their children a culture and societal order that must be strictly adhered to. Wealth is power, and power is revered, and the Rivingtons preached this to their children with religious zeal. Such a pretentious world can only develop hollow hearts and brazen egos; traits naturally inherited by Chet and Rosemary.

Chet, the only male heir of the house, was afforded more liberties to challenge the limits of their societal rules. He once was driving while drunk and badly injured another motorist. Threats of criminal prosecution and civil lawsuits were quickly extinguished by the payment of the right amount of money. The only lesson Chet learned that day was how easy it can be to pay his way out of trouble. Contrarily, as the youngest and only daughter, Rosemary was strictly protected, and more was demanded of her. Such oversight was purposeful. It was intended to teach her the importance of being a guardian of the family name, a role she readily adopted as she was never loathe to report any of Chet's wrongdoings to her parents. For years, the Rivington family existed in this pretentious world, governed by steep social hierarchies, and a powerful system of checks and balances.

The Rivington mansion is a 9,200 square foot Victorian style estate, complete with thirty rooms, a large library, and an office. A home of this size necessitated the need for many servants. Butlers, maids, chefs, and groundskeepers lived near, working at the home year round. For the Rivingtons, it was the royalty they deserved. For the servants, it was a very demanding occupation. The pay was excellent, but the strict demands of the family and their stuffy personalities always made for an overbearing environment.

In the Rivington household, there are rules; strict rules never to be broken. The first was that all domestic servants hired must be non-white. Only people of African-American or Spanish heritage were hired. The discriminatory practice of hiring only minorities to clean the house and cook the meals was meant to enforce the social and racial order that their family has always aspired to; one that forever perpetuates their overarching societal caste system over the poor minority class. Of course, the days of slavery were long gone, and these servants could come and go as freely as they wished. However, to these workers the financial security of such an occupation was far greater than they could ever hope to find elsewhere, forcing them to endure the insufferable conditions.

The Rivington household has one other main rule; one which

is absolutely unfathomable to violate. That rule is that none of the Rivington family, friends, and guests are allowed to fraternize with the staff. Of course, it was acceptable to be polite to the workers at the home. This rule instead was crystal clear to all in that there was no greater sin that could occur in the Rivington household than to be romantically involved with, or have sexual relations with, any of the staff. This was a rule that clearly challenged the 18 year old playboy Chet from the first moment he saw the newly hired maid at the estate; a lovely 20 year old Puerto Rican woman.

# Embark

I am blessed to live in a building with a tight knit community of friends who are always eager to help each other. Lucy Fallock is one such friend. In her mid-60's, Lucy is a widower, retiree, and most of all, an animal lover. Years ago, she successfully spearheaded a campaign to derail a plan by the Board of Trustees of our building, which sought to implement a policy that forbids occupants from having pets.

Lucy, who currently has one cat, one dog, a fish, and a hamster, is always eager to look after Clubber when I'm away. For her, watching my large golden retriever was a joy. For me, it was relief to give comfort to a dog whose breed is known for craving constant companionship. So when I knocked on her door to call on her services once again, Lucy was more than happy to oblige as Clubber marched right in to his awaiting friends.

My journey to the North Fork region was traversed via the infamous Long Island Expressway, which on this particular day, the traffic was surprisingly modest, and the ride only took about two hours. Long Island has always been synonymous with beaches and strip malls, but the North Fork is different. Trips here usually leave visitors breathless. While not as chic as its counterpart to the South, the North Fork is a fascinating mix of farm country, vineyards, beaches, and estuaries, all of which offer a never-ending breath of fresh air for locals and visitors alike. The Forks are divided by the Peconic Bay.

Settled in the 1600's by Puritan farmers, the history of the

North Fork is as rich as its fertile soil that bountifully yields many crops. In the early 1900's, farmers tried their hand in growing tobacco, with some success. Later, European immigrants brought with them their knowledge of growing potatoes and cauliflower to add to the other predominant crops yielded in this region. In the 1970's, many of the rich parcels of land began to transition from growing vegetables to grapes, thus giving rise to the vast vineyards that exist today.

The North Fork is comprised of several hamlets, including the town of Orient, which is the eastern most part of Long Island approximately 105 miles east of New York City. It is also the place where Maria Cruz was murdered 37 years ago. The other hamlets in the North Fork region include East Marion, Greenport, Southold, Peconic, Cutchogue, Mattituck, and Laurel. They are each blessed with a small town charm boasting country stores, antique shops, fruit and vegetable stands, and a variety of restaurants.

Many families have called the North Fork area their home for centuries, perfectly content with enjoying their days in this bucolic bliss. Over the years, an influx of new inhabitants from the New York area joined the lifelong residents in this region to make it their second home, and eventually their permanent residence.

Riverhead lies approximately 25 miles west of the North Fork hamlets. This is the last and largest commercial area before venturing into the smaller hamlets and tranquil countryside. Boasting the largest library in the area, Riverhead was my first destination. After scoffing down a burger and fries at a local diner, a friendly waitress informed me that the library was just three blocks down passed the church over on Main Street. After paying the check, I made my way eager to begin my search.

The Riverhead Public Library is a large brick structure surrounded by decorative glass. On this particular day, there were only a few patrons, and it felt like it was my own private library. The very friendly staff greeted me and offered full access to all the available services. The microfilm machines are housed on the lower level of the library. The staff instructed me how to load the spools of film for viewing. A large computer monitor displayed the images with vivid clarity, and after finally figuring out how to configure the page layout for proper viewing, my search began.

I sat comfortably in my own personal carrel in the lower level of this very quiet library with the complete reels of all the *Long Island Sound* publications spanning from to April 1959 to December 1984. My search immediately narrowed to publications beginning on October 1, 1972. The first article I could find covering the murder was the same October 21, 1972 article that I saw in my laundry library. Just to be sure, I compared it to the picture taken on my cell phone and they matched.

I then began the arduous task of carefully reviewing each subsequent edition. The next article relating to the story was on the fifth page of the October 26, 1972 edition of the *Long Island Sound*, but it was largely a rehashing of the original story printed in the preceding Saturday edition. As with the first, the second article was authored by a reporter named George McBride. A few more articles appeared within the next two weeks, but nothing substantially new was reported on the case. Then an article appeared on October 31st that identified Detective John Conte as the lead investigator in the case. It contained a few crime scene photos of the location where the body was found, but nothing different from the previous articles.

For nearly three hours, my search through the *Long Island Sound* catalogue, and all other area publications, produced no other information on the story. Growing fatigued, I walked away from the carrel to rest my weary eyes for a few moments and visited a nearby deli for some coffee and a snack before resuming my search. Now feeling refreshed, I began a more methodical search and found, on page 2 of the November 30th edition, a story headlined

*"Lead Detective of the Maria Cruz Murder Case Resigns."*

The article read:

*"John Conte of the Southold Police Force and lead investigator of the*

*Maria Cruz murder has resigned from the force. Department officials refused to comment on the story or the status of any of the cases he had been investigating."*

Without more information, it was difficult to understand why the lead investigator of the case abruptly resigned. Like the others, this latest article was authored by George McBride. Other than the murder victim, he was the only common thread in this story. A quick internet search yielded some useful information on this reporter. Although retired as a reporter, he still resides and works in the area, offering random editorials and travel advice for a local travel agency in the nearby hamlet of Peconic, New York. Having exhausted my review of the only articles seemingly ever written about the murder of Maria Cruz, it appeared that the only way for me to start piecing together this fragmented story was to go right to the closest source possible, George McBride.

# Empathy

Lola Cruz had always been an excellent student; an avid learner who thrived while receiving a modest education. Having excelled in public elementary and middle schools, she earned her high school diploma from Seward Park High School in New York City. She regularly met with the school guidance counselors to discuss future opportunities. Going to college had always been a dream, but without opportunities for scholarships, and no real means to finance a higher education, Lola always knew that it was an unrealistic goal. This dream grew even more remote when Lita's health began to deteriorate. So before Lola even graduated high school, she was forced to begin work to provide for her ailing Grandmother.

Lola has always felt blessed to have a strong work ethic and high level of resourcefulness. These traits, coupled with her natural wit and pleasant demeanor, led to many job opportunities, some of which were fairly lucrative. While still in high school, Lola entered into a *"Job/Shop"* program where students would attend school one week, and the next week would work at a job offering valuable life skills experience. Her first job in this program was working as a data processor in a small firm in the World Trade Center. After earning a high school diploma, Lola landed a position as a personal assistant to a partner in an accounting firm. Here she learned to budget the demanding needs of a professional in a fast moving environment. Despite the frantic pace, Lola enjoyed the work, and excelled at it.

Several years after Lita's death, Lola began working in a prominent bank in New York City. She started as a bank teller, working her way up through the ranks until landing the Branch Manager position, supervising a large group of bank employees, and overseeing a wide array of banking transactions on a daily basis. She often recalls the first time she spent inside the bank's vault. Despite being in the same room with more money than most people have ever known or cared to imagine, to Lola, the smell of the cache of currency was "ugly." Since much of her life was spent just above the poverty line, Lola was raised to appreciate the value of things, not the amount of them, and this taught her to live within limited means.

At the bank, Lola took comfort from the busy workload and decent pay, but in reality, dealing with the varied personalities that would enter the branch on a daily basis to handle their financial transactions was truly the most satisfying part. Lola had gotten to know personally the many bank customers, and enjoyed working with and befriending them.

On this particular day, a coworker named Eloise was assisting Gladys Ford and her son Michael, a new customer who on this day sought to open up a checking account and rent a safe deposit box. It was among the many services provided by the bank. Lola sat at her desk and watched painfully as the young son berated his mother for taking too long with the paperwork. The poor elderly woman fumbled for her reading glasses as the impatient and seemingly embarrassed son was rushing the process.

Lola thought back to her youth sitting at the dining room table assisting Lita with important documents, the payment of bills, and other items. Lola always diligently helped in this way, not only from devotion to her loving Grandmother, but also because Lita was illiterate.

Lita's inability to read or write was not surprising. After all, she was forced to work her entire life leaving no time for Lita to attend school. Many other similarly situated adults probably shared the same sad fate, but no one ever spoke of such things, and there was a firm understanding between them that they would always keep Lita's illiteracy a secret.

As Lita aged, she became increasingly unwilling to try to learn how to read and write. Still, Lola did her best to teach Lita to identify and even write simple words, while simultaneously taking every opportunity to fiercely protect their secret from being exposed. One Christmas, when Lola was quite young, a child of some visiting relatives asked Lita to read a holiday card out loud. Although fully immersed in the opening of her presents, Lola rushed over to assist Lita by offering to read it herself. Her youthful exuberance saved the day as Lola read the card and Lita's secret was protected. Such support systems are likely very important among families dealing with illiteracy, where unspoken codes are developed and utilized to mask the dark shame felt by both the one who is illiterate and the family members concealing it.

Lita used her illiteracy as motivation to instill in Lola an incredibly strong work ethic. She also saw to it that her Granddaughter received the best education possible so that she would never suffer a similar plight. Lola came to understand Lita's motivation, and had never forgotten her for it.

And now, as the young Mr. Ford pounded on the table with his fists in frustration at his mother's inability to comprehend or perhaps even read the paperwork, Lola approached the table to offer some assistance. The young man pouted as the mother pleaded for help with desperate eyes. Lola asked Eloise to escort Mr. Ford for some coffee and pastries provided by the bank as she calmed the shaken woman, who placed her soft hand in Lola's hand and thanked her.

"No worries, Mrs. Ford," said a smiling Lola. "This is a difficult process, so we'll just take our time."

# Scoop

George McBride had always fancied himself as a hard-nosed reporter. His journalism career began with the *New York Tribune*, a small publication in Queens, New York just outside of Manhattan. Like any young reporter, he hit the ground running, forever in search of the big scoop; a story so juicy that would catapult him into stardom. Although a good writer and full of integrity, he never found that scoop. Over the years, the zeal tempered, causing a search for a much-needed change. A distant family member shared the availability of a position with the *Long Island Sound*, a local newspaper dedicated to "*The life and times of the North Fork*," and after much thought, George McBride relocated to the serene North Fork area in 1970. Two years later, the death of Maria Cruz landed him the scoop he waited for his entire career, or so it seemed.

I called George at the travel agency in Peconic to discuss the nature of my research, and after a short discussion, we agreed to meet him at his home office in Cutchogue within the hour. George lived in a small ranch home that doubled as a home office, complete with an antique writer's desk and several large file cabinets. He regaled me with tales from the old days where he "made his bones" in Queens, New York. When I told him that I lived in Sunnyside, he fondly recalled visiting the former boxing arena that used to be on 45th street at Queens Boulevard.

"Those were the days. I miss the action that comes from being near the big bad city. Coming out here was almost like retiring," he said with a chuckle. "Seriously, there are good people here, and it is generally quiet. The only action usually comes during the tourist season. You know, drunk drivers, theft allegations at the estates. Minor stuff like that mostly."

I immediately took a liking to George. Although a bit rough around the edges, he was beaming with pride, and it was clear that his enthusiasm for reporting was still prevalent. I asked George if he has any recollection of the Maria Cruz murder and the articles he wrote in the *Long Island Sound* long ago.

"Sure, I remember that case," he said after bellowing a loud smoker's cough. "What a tragedy that was."

"Can you tell me more about it?" I asked.

"Well," he replied, "there was not much more to go on other than what was printed. The body was found savagely stabbed and wrapped in plastic. Coroner thinks she was killed sometime in late September and buried for a couple of weeks before the body was found."

"How was her body found?" I asked.

"A call came into the police and they were on it pretty quick. I was having breakfast at a diner when an officer got a first call. A tall cop named Conte, John Conte. I overheard the details on his police radio, and he ran out ahead of me and I followed close behind. That's how I was, always looking for that scoop" he fondly recalled before continuing.

"Anyway, Conte got there and started to cordon off the area. There were a bunch of kids playing in the field. They smelled a foul odor and told their parents about it and they called the police."

"One of your articles reported that officer Conte was in charge of the investigation. Was that right?" I asked.

"Yes, at first," he replied. "He was a good cop. He came from Brooklyn a year or two before the murder. Everyone liked him. But over time, his role in the investigation was slowly diminished until he was removed from the case entirely."

"What was the reason for that?" I asked.

"I'm not sure. The department claimed that he wasn't producing answers fast enough," he said with a dismissive look on his face.

"Did you believe that?" I asked.

"That was a bunch of baloney," he replied. "He was working as hard as he could, and had no help whatsoever."

I asked who replaced him and without hesitation, he replied "Luther Vale."

"Was Mr. Vale more experienced?" I asked.

"Hell no", he retorted. "Vale was a dipshit schmoozer who had his nose up everyone's ass. But he was a tough bastard. A big guy who put a lot of fear into people. He made his way up the ladder in a really short time. He was connected somehow. There was a rumor going around that he was hooked up with the Rivington family over on Shelter Island."

"Hooked up?" I asked.

"Something about him moonlighting as their private security or something" he replied. "It was all kept under wraps, but I heard things. A good reporter always does. Here's something else you should know. Chet, the youngest son of the Rivington family, was rumored to have had an affair with the murder victim about a year before she turned up dead."

"Why wasn't that in any of your articles?" I asked.

"I tried digging into that rumor, but I could only scratch the surface. Then, out of the blue, my editor forced me to abandon that part of the story entirely and to stick with the crime alone. As for Conte, I can tell you that he was making progress. He was knocking on doors, trying to gather evidence. He was the one who was able to identify Maria's body. If not, they probably would have never known who she was. Once Vale took over the case, every-thing got shutdown. The story got cold and then died altogether."

"What was the town's reaction?" I asked.

"Initially, they were all up in arms" he replied, "but as time passed the story faded, and lives went on as usual. As for Vale, he got a raise and remained on the force for many years. Today he lives off a fat pension and serves as a Trustee in the Town of

Southold."

"What about Conte?" I asked.

"That is a sad story" he replied. "After he was removed from the case, there were rumblings of some trouble he had back in Brooklyn before coming here. He was facing charges or something, and was forced to leave in shame. Some shit that Luther Vale was leaking to my editor, I think. Since I was told to only report on the crime, I refused to report it. Besides, it sounded like a smear campaign to me. So Conte just got up and left the force and never looked back."

"Do you know where he went?" I asked.

George scratched his head in thought, stood up, and went to check in a metal file cabinet. After a few minutes, he pulled out a folder and opened it.

"Here it is, he moved to a small town in upstate New York. Last known address is 1000 Pauley Lane, Deposit, New York. That is a world away from here. I tried reaching out to him after he left, but he was in no mood to hear from anyone in this area."

I scribbled down the address in my notepad.

"George, were there any possible witnesses to the crime?" I asked.

"Not really, unless you consider Margaret Taves. She was known by everyone in the area as 'Crazy Maggie'," he said with a chuckle that made his bloated belly shake.

"She was a hoot all right. She lived out in Orient, alone in a small house. She never recovered from the loss of her husband who died one night in his sleep. She had one kid, but he went away somewhere out west, and she was left all alone. That is when she really began to do things that made people around here think she was crazy."

George reclined in his seat to reflect before continuing,

"Maggie would sit motionless for hours each night by her front window with newspaper clippings of the assassination of President John F. Kennedy taped onto the glass. I drove by one night to see it for myself. If you can believe it, she sat in this big chair just staring into the distance out her front window covered with these news articles. In the window, there were three bullet holes in the glass right where her head was. Till this day, I still don't know if they were real bullet holes, or if the holes were drilled, but it was creepy nonetheless. It got to be such a scene that the local kids would get together in front of her house drinking beer and whooping it up at Crazy Maggie. All kidding aside, I actually felt bad for the woman. She had mental illness before it was properly diagnosed, and those around her had little tolerance or understanding of it."

"She kept to herself mostly and this also made people think she was crazy. She lived alone with a bunch of cats and she was never known to have any visitors. At night, she went on long walks in the dark. Have you seen how dark it can be at night out there in Orient? Hell, it's in the middle of nowhere. She lived right near where Maria's body was found, you know. Anyway, the rumor at the time was that Maggie may have seen something on the night of the murder, but nothing ever came of it."

"George, are there are any markings of the exact location where the body was found?"

"Kid," he said, "you'll never find it if you tried." He looked at his watch and said "Tell you what, give me five minutes to finish this letter I have to mail and I will take you out there myself and show you the exact spot."

"I can't thank you enough, George," I said.

"Don't mention it, kid."

A short while later, I followed George in his old brown and white Chrysler LeBaron on the twenty mile ride to the precise location of where Maria's body was found. We drove through the tranquil hamlet of Orient filled with stunning wildlife, spacious farms, protected marshlands, and rocky beaches. Various homes were spread out within this area, many with signs that read "*Posted; No Trespassing*."

We turned off Route 25 in Orient, traveling along a winding

and narrow paved road for about two miles, before stopping at an intersection of several adjacent fields. Nearby, the waves of Hallock's Bay rolled melodically onto the rocky coastline not far from the Orient Beach State Park and the Long Beach Bar Lighthouse, otherwise known as the "Bug Lighthouse." I admired the vast swaths of land, which as George explained, is mostly owned by the New York State Department of Conservation who purchased it for preservation purposes.

With George leading the way, we walked about 200 yards into the field. I continuously scanned the scenery and could see a twenty-foot high wooden platform aerie that hosted several osprey chicks.

"Those birds are fish hawks," he said. "They are native to the area. The local bird enthusiasts have been building platforms like this all over the area for several years now. It makes a nice nesting area for the birds, who have made a comeback since they banned that nasty insecticide DDT."

I continued to study the land as George, who was now breathing heavy from the walk, slowed his pace. Approximately fifty feet to the right of the aerie are four trees with each one larger than the other spanning from left to right. After a small break in the trees, there is a thicker set of trees to the right, and beyond that, you can spot the shimmering waves of the bay. George pointed to a spot directly in front of the largest tree.

"There," he said. "They found her body in a grave right in front of that largest tree. The tree was a lot smaller back then, but that's the exact spot."

As I approached, I shuddered to think that I was looking at the exact location where Maria Cruz was murdered and buried in a shallow grave 37 years ago. The few pictures that were published of this place did nothing to capture the eeriness I now felt while standing here. George made the sign of the cross and said a brief prayer as I looked around in amazement at the size and serenity of the field. It was clear that this location was chosen by a killer who was cunning enough to know that out here, no one would have seen this heinous act taking place. My focus returned back to the burial site, and other than a few random rocks and seashells scattered about, there was nothing to indicate the horror that was committed in such a peaceful place so long ago.

The nearest house was about three hundred yards to the west. George pointed to it and told me that was where Crazy Maggie lived.

"She died some time last year," he said. "The locals complained of a foul smell coming from her home and called the police to investigate. Upon entry, they discovered Maggie's body lying peacefully in her bed. The coroner's report said that she had been dead for nearly a month before her body was found. She left what little she had to her son."

"George, can you tell me more about the alleged affair between Maria and Chet Rivington?"

"All I have ever heard was that they were having an affair about a year before she was killed when she was working as a maid at the Rivington estate. I used to snoop around town and ask questions, but I was never able to confirm it. All I've ever heard were whispers from some of the older folk, but they were like a secret society. And with the Rivingtons involved, nobody wanted to talk."

I continued to jot down the information relayed to me when George said, "Hey kid, I've got to ask. Why do you care so much about this case?"

"Truth be told," I replied, "I believe that there is more to this story. This poor woman died in this lonely place a long time ago and her murder was never solved. It's a damn shame. So, why do I care so much? Let's just call it a need to know."

He shook his head in agreement and said, "You may be right, but it was so long ago. You're probably chasing a ghost now. But if you want to start somewhere, you should start with Conte, if he's still alive. And if I were you, I would stay away from Vale. I never trusted that son of a bitch. The way I see it, he did nothing but impede the investigation."

I smiled and thanked him for his help and his advice.

He nodded proudly as he removed an old business card from his wallet and handed it to me.

"If you find anything" George said, "or have any other questions, just give me a call."

We shook hands. He had a sincere look in his eye and I could tell that he still cared about this case. It was as if the reporter in him had been reborn, and this story was the scoop he had longed for his entire life, but never achieved.

"Oh, one other thing", he said. "Pay a visit over at the Oyster Cove Inn in Greenport. Maria worked there and that was the last place she was seen alive. I know the owners there, they are good people."

I thanked him again as we both made our way back to our cars.

# Pariah

Margaret Bixby Connor Taves was born and raised in Orient, New York. Known as Maggie to many of her friends, she was an aspiring artist and nature lover, who cherished the countryside near her home. As she aged, Maggie became a recluse up until her death in 2008.

For her entire life Maggie struggled with a mental illness that today would be properly diagnosed as Bipolar Disorder, but during much of her lifetime, it was known as Manic Depression. Before it was correctly diagnosed, and without adequate funding for treatment, sufferers of this condition had serious struggles. And Maggie was no exception. She was ridiculed in school by her peers, and punished by her strict parents and unforgiving teachers who had no tolerance for her condition, all of which left Maggie to be shunned publicly. Throughout the years, bouts with her mental illness spawned the nickname "Crazy Maggie."

Desperate for love, Maggie married a local fisherman named Stu Peters when she was just 19 years old. She endured a very rocky relationship and several beatings before Peters left home never to return. Years later, Maggie met John Taves, a Vietnam War veteran who struggled with Post Traumatic Stress Disorder after his years of service. After a brief courtship, the two were married a short time later. Maggie and John moved into the home where Maggie was raised, and to the shock of everyone, the couple enjoyed a happy life together. They shared a common love for photography and nature, both of which were in ample supply in the North Fork and very therapeutic for both of their respective conditions.

Several years later, Maggie gave birth to the couple's first and only child, a boy they named Hatcher. The couple enjoyed raising their son in Orient until John's untimely death from a massive heart attack when Hatcher was still a teenager. After graduating high school, Hatcher relocated to the west coast to attend college, leaving Maggie to spend the remainder of her days alone in Orient.

Weeks after the body of Maria Cruz was found, there were rumblings of a potential witness to the crime, and Luther Vale was eager to pay his old friend Maggie a visit. He had long been the regular responder to many calls from Maggie who reported strangers creeping near her home during all hours of the night. Luther would stop by her house to take the report, and to help himself to whatever was available in the refrigerator. It was a far greater routine that he would have liked. But on this night, Luther had a sinister motive; to make sure that Maggie *saw* nothing.

Maggie stood outside her back door wearing an old nightgown, white socks, and slippers. She was calling for Boobie and Whiskers, two of her cats that snuck out the door while she was taking out the trash. Maggie Taves loved her cats. Six in all; they were rescues, but in her mind, they rescued her from loneliness and despair. When she would go into a psychotic episode, her cats would help soothe her until it passed.

Luther approached from behind her and said, "Hello Maggie."

"What do you want? I didn't call. Is something wrong?" said Maggie frantically.

"Calm down Maggie. I just want to talk" replied Luther as he walked into the house ahead of her and sat at the kitchen table.

Longing to retrieve her cats, she knew not to keep him waiting, so she followed into the kitchen leaving the door slightly ajar.

"What are you doing Maggie? I hear that you are going around saying you saw something relating to that woman killed out in the field," Luther snorted.

Maggie was a sufferer of mental illness, but she was by no

means dim-witted. She read clearly the ominous tone of his words.

"Oh, that was nothing" she said. "Some young cop was asking questions." She opened a cabinet drawer to retrieve a business card he left her and said, "It was this guy Conte."

"What did you tell him Maggie?" snapped Luther.

"I told him that I thought I saw something out in the fields on that night."

"What did you say you saw Maggie?" he barked.

"Just people walking around. The same I always say that I see Luther. Don't mind it. I was having another episode. I told him that," she said in fear.

"Maggie, you know that no one is going to believe an old crazy coot like you right? I mean, you always say you see something that doesn't exist."

Maggie nodded affirmatively hoping to appease him into leaving. She sat back down at the table, clutched the lower fringes of her nightgown, and stared down submissively at the floor.

"Maggie, look at me," commanded Luther in a stern tone causing her immediately to meet his eyes. "If I hear you saying another peep, I will have you taken away."

Tears began to well in her eyes and she twirled her hair frantically. He knew that her greatest fear was being committed to an insane asylum.

"That's right Maggie. Locked up in the crazy house with the other crazies. Then, your son would have to come back and take care of your things here. And your cats, oh my, they would be taken to the pound and euthanized, that is unless they have their little necks snapped first. Am I making myself clear Maggie?"

"Yes sir," said Maggie. "Please don't do that, sir. I have nothing to report. I promise you."

Satisfied with his dominance over her, Luther stood and grabbed a banana from the counter and peeled it. He took a bite and tossed the remainder of it on the kitchen table in front of her.

"It was nice to visit you tonight Maggie. We'll talk soon," he said.

As he neared the door, the cats had returned and Luther bent down to pick one of them up.

"They are so cute," he said coldly. "It would be a damn shame if anything happened to them."

He placed the cat down on the floor and exited the home. Maggie bolted the door behind him, shut off the lights, and crouched in the corner of her kitchen floor. As she sat in the dark, Whiskers came to her lap and she hugged him tightly. Thoughts of being locked up in an insane asylum, causing pain to her son, and endangering the lives of her precious babies was too much to bear. Frozen in fear, Maggie remained in that panicked state for several hours as the world was closing in.

# Forgotten By Time

Approximately ten miles west of Orient lay Greenport, the largest of the North Fork hamlets. This quaint town boasts a rich maritime history, particularly because it was a large whaling port and a popular launching point for many sailing events. The opening of the railroad in the mid 1800's caused a huge boom to this area for those seeking work or leisure.

Today, with a population of over 2,000 residents, Greenport is a bustling town and a thriving tourist destination for many North Fork vacationers. The town has several hotels, some of which are quite swanky. There are many trendy shops selling high-end fashion clothing, jewelry, and souvenirs. Visitors with fancy palates are treated to the many fine seafood eateries and other varied restaurants serving a myriad of delicacies. The town also has a carousel that is well over 100 years old, set in the center of a large park near a busy pier with many places to relax and take in the town's charm.

A few miles from the center of town lies the Oyster Cove Inn, a sleepy beachfront property with small cottages and motel rooms nestled on several acres of waterfront property. Driving into the property, you can't help but notice the distinctive, and apparently the original neon sign, adorned with the Inn's logo of a mermaid in a seashell. This place seems completely forgotten by time, with a never-ending appeal to those that are lucky enough to know of it. It was also the last place that Maria Cruz was seen alive.

I turned into the property's long graveled driveway and parked near the entrance. As I entered the lobby, Laura Wendt, the owner of the Inn, greeted me. The Wendt family first opened the establishment in the 1950's to be passed down through the family for generations. Laura is a pleasant woman who grew up living and working at the Inn. Now in her late 60's, she is current owner and manager of the Oyster Cove Inn who is constantly turning away would-be investors seeking to purchase the property from her and build up on its rustic charm. Laura was more than eager to speak with me about Maria.

"Sure, I remember her," she said. "She worked with us on and off for about a year, mostly doing housekeeping duties and so forth. She was always pleasant, respectful and very responsible. Once, she overheard one of the guests saying that they needed milk. So, during a work break, she went to pick some up for them. The family was so pleased at this kind gesture and it reflected well for our business. You don't see that every day with an employee."

"Were you here the night she went missing? I asked.

"Yes," she replied. "She worked until about 10 pm. It's always real quiet here at night, and I didn't hear anything. The next day I saw her car parked in the lot, but she wasn't scheduled to work. I thought she may have switched with another worker, but that wasn't the case, as all our staff was accounted for. Her car sat parked there for several days and since she stopped showing up for work, I got worried, so I called the police."

"What type of car did she drive?" I asked.

"I think it was a blue Chevy Nova." she replied.

"Do you remember who you spoke to when you reported her missing?" I asked.

"No, but after Maria's body was found, Detective Conte came over to inspect the car. As I understand it, they were able to find fingerprints in the car that matched samples taken from the body found in the field. He also asked for pictures of Maria to confirm her identity, which he took with him."

"Did Mr. Conte come back to speak with you and your staff?" I asked.

"No," she replied.

"How about Luther Vale? Did he come by here?"

"No," she replied again. "No one came back."

I was puzzled as to why Luther, or anyone from the police department, never followed up to investigate the last place that Maria was seen alive.

Then with a sad expression on her face, Laura said, "It was such a terrible thing to happen to a sweet girl like Maria. And her poor little girl. What a sin."

"Little girl?" I asked.

"Oh yes, Maria had a daughter, a little girl named Lola. She was the sweetest thing ever. She brought her around here a couple of times. She had to be no more than a few months old when Maria died."

I was stunned by this revelation. If Maria had a daughter, why was it never reported? What happened to this child? If she's alive, does she know the fate of her poor mother? And does she know the identity of her father? These questions bounced around in my brain like a pinball.

I asked Laura if she knew who the father could be.

"I've heard the rumors of her going with that philandering bastard, Chet Rivington" she replied. "He tossed girls away like people throw out the trash. I am sure that he had his hands on her. Maria was very beautiful."

"Do you believe that Maria and Chet were in a relationship?" I asked.

"I can't say for sure. Maria was very responsible, but he was handsome, rich, and had a lot of power. And where there's smoke there's fire. Rumors like that don't just pop up out of nowhere. I know that she was close to one of her co-workers at the Rivington estate, Ginny Foster. You can check with her. She's retired now and lives in Greenport."

Laura jotted down Ginny's phone number on a card and passed it to me.

I then asked Laura if she knew what might have happened to the baby after Maria died.

"Unfortunately no," she said. "They lived in a small apartment in town and her Grandmother watched the baby while Maria worked."

"Have you heard from the Grandmother?" I asked.

"No" she replied, "But I think Maria also had some family or friends who lived in the city somewhere."

She went into the back room and returned with a metal box containing a stack of index cards and said, "We keep the contact information for all our employees."

Laura flipped through the index cards then paused and said, "I am not sure if I should give you this information. Are you a detective or something?"

"No Laura, I am not. I am an attorney who stumbled onto the story of Maria's death. I am just trying to get to the bottom of this case. And now that I know that Maria had a daughter, I would like to try to find her and share with her what I have found."

Laura looked me and with a wink said, "Well I cannot personally give this to you, but I have to make a quick telephone call in the back room. Please excuse me."

Laura left the index card on the desk and detecting her ruse, I quickly jotted down the information while she was gone. The card read: *Nadia Lopez, 90 Baruch Street, Apartment #5C, New York, NY.* When she returned, I asked Laura if there was a vacancy at the Inn.

"Sure," she said. "We have a small cottage near the water. How long do you need it for?"

"I may be here a while," I said with a smile.

Laura handed me the key and directed me to my cottage.

After settling in, I sat in front of my cottage overlooking the water studying Maria's contact information. Could this be the place where Maria's daughter was taken after her death? At the very least, would someone there know of her whereabouts? If Maria's daughter was still alive, she would probably be about 38 years old. Would she even know about her mother's death, or is it shrouded in mystery?

These swirling questions posed a serious dilemma. Should I try to contact a woman who may have gone her whole life without knowing what happened to her mother? I would not be able to forgive myself if I cause nothing but unfounded pain for this poor woman. Yet, if she is unaware of her mother's fate, how do I refrain from telling her anything that could shed light on that great mystery?

I decided that the responsible thing to do before attempting to contact Lola is to wait and see if I can uncover enough evidence that would give cause to reopen the case. And the only person I knew who could help me with that is my old law school pal turned federal prosecutor, Andre Carter.

# Longing

He carefully placed a long line of cocaine onto the stomach of the young stripper sleeping next to him after the two spent another long night of partying together. He admired her toned muscles for a moment before snorting the powder, which jolted his brain like a lightning bolt. He then traced the same path up her stomach with his tongue. The two have been on a non-stop bender for two straight days. For a man in his mid-50's he is generally in good health, but his rampant use of cocaine and alcohol threatened to undermine that.

The morning sun beamed into the bedroom of his luxurious apartment off Central Park. He despised it, but he knew he had to rise for a teleconference scheduled in the next hour for some random business deal with his partners in Amsterdam. Such multi-million dollar deals became relatively normal over the years for his private equity firm. He arose from his bed and took a moment to stretch. He again studied the naked body of his sultry escort as she rolled over onto her stomach exposing her firm and perfectly shaped buttocks, and large rose shaped tattoo on her back. That is a world class ass, he pleasantly thought. However, it wasn't difficult to curtail his arousement. They've had so much sex over the past few days that his usual morning erection was nonexistent.

He made a slow but steady walk across the cold floor tiled with luxurious Italian marble. As with everything he owns, it is the best that money can buy. Although his apartment had four large bedrooms, he only used the master bedroom for rest and pleasure.

As he neared the bathroom towards the rear, he stopped by the smallest bedroom and turned on the light. It was painted white, and completely empty. In a perfect world, it would be decorated lavishly and occupied by the one person in the world he would never know, his daughter. He knew that she would have loved the life he could have provided for her. She would have attended the finest schools, travelled the world, and enjoyed the best of everything. But that was not to be.

These moments always caused him to think about Maria. It's been almost 40 years since they've been together, and he still yearns for her. He has often wondered how different his life would have been had they remained together. Yes, he would still be rich, but his heart would also be full with love, instead of the empty chasm it is today. If they were together, he would have a loving family, and not have to rely upon paid escorts to act the part. Wealth has its benefits, he thought, as he looked back towards his bed to see the tattooed back of his lovely escort laying in a deep slumber. But can it buy happiness? He has sure spent his life trying without success. Waving these thoughts away, he shut the light off in the room and quickly showered.

Dressed casually, he sat at his desk and joined the teleconference from his computer. He sat quietly as attorneys spoke in both English and Dutch finalizing the details of the transaction

Upon completing the deal, his partner said, "It's a pleasure doing business with you, Mr. Rivington."

"Dankjewel," he said in his finest Dutch accent and finished with "And please feel free to call me Chet" before exiting the call.

As he arose, Chet noticed the light on in the back bedroom. Strange, he thought. He swore he shut that light off before showering. He walked over to give it a quick look. The room was empty as always. He turned off the light, removed his clothes, and returned to wake up his lovely escort for some more partying.

# Home Cooking

Despite having just devoured a huge lunch, the smell of apple pie permeating throughout the small apartment made my mouth water.

"I try to make pie at least once a week," said Virginia Foster. "It keeps me sharp."

Known as Ginny, Mrs. Foster is a tall, somewhat obese, African American woman in her early 70's. She is a pleasant woman with a bright smile and smooth voice that charmed the room. For more than 25 years, Ginny was the main cook at the Rivington estate. As she got older, her health began to wane, forcing her to retire and settle in a small apartment in Greenport, New York. When I telephoned her and explained how I just met with Laura, she was more than happy to meet with me.

"I worked at the Rivington's for many years," said Ginny. "I kept to myself, did my work diligently, and I advised everyone who came to work after me to do the same."

"What was it like working there?" I asked.

"It wasn't easy, I'll tell you that. Miss Sarah ruled the home with an iron fist."

"Sarah Rivington, Chet's mother?" I asked, and Ginny nodded.

"I often stayed clear of her. Mr. Rivington, though, he was a bit more compassionate. And Rosemary, their daughter, she had a forked tongue, that one. Like I said, I just kept my head down and did my work."

"What about Chet?" I asked.

"Oh, he was a smooth one, that boy. He had all the ladies look-ing at him. I never spoke much to either of the children."

"Do you remember when Maria started?" I asked.

"Yes, she replied. "It must have been around 1970. A fine young woman she was. She was a maid and did all the cleaning and other household chores. Pretty girl, too. I knew that there would be a set of eyes on her."

I asked if there was any truth to the rumors of an affair be-tween Maria and Chet.

"I never saw anything," she replied, "but the rules of the house were clear."

"Rules?" I asked.

"Oh yes," she replied. "Nobody from staff was allowed to go with anyone from the house. Miss Sarah and Mr. Rivington al-ways went on and on about that rule. It was the law as far as we were concerned, and they put the fear of God into everyone in the house not to break it. Like I said, I never saw anything happen, but I did see how Chet and Maria looked at each other. I warned the girl how risky it was. She denied anything, but a lady knows. That boy was after her something fierce."

"Do you remember the day you found out Maria was killed?" I asked.

"Oh, how terrible. It was about three weeks after they found her body. Police came around to ask us all a bunch of questions" she replied.

"I have yet to meet Mr. Conte," I said as I took out his picture given to me by George to confirm his identity.

She looked at it and said, "I was not interviewed by anyone named Conte."

Surprised, I asked, "Who did interview you?"

"Luther Vale," she quickly replied. "That fellow came around the house asking questions. I thought that was strange because Mr. Vale was always around the house. I'd seen him at parties, meet-ings, and other events. He was very close to the Rivingtons. I could swear that he worked for them or something, and here he was flashing a police badge and asking questions about Maria's murder."

I was always bothered by the conflict in having an officer, who is a close friend of the family, questioning them about this murder. But until now, I had no idea how close this Mr. Vale was to the Rivington family, and that made it all the more suspicious.

Sensing her fatigue from our discussion, I stood and said, "Ginny, I've already taken up enough of your time. Thank you for your help."

"My pleasure dear," she said. "May God have mercy on Maria's soul. I will say a special prayer for her in church on Sunday."

# Patrol

Bobby Manfredi loved exploring the wooded areas of Shelter Island. To a ten year old boy, this was his forest; one to explore and conquer. He was too young to join his father on his annual big game hunting trips, which this season promised to produce a record harvest. To fill that void, Bobby went on his own to "harvest" whatever adventure he could find. With him was his trusted companion Roxy, a scruffy tan and white mixed terrier. The two often sought adventure in these woods chasing squirrels and the occasional deer. Bobby fashioned his mother's old sheet into a cape, and fixed an undersized shirt on Roxy.

As they ventured deeper into the forest, Bobby scaled a small man-made stone wall. He reached back to lift his tiny companion over the wall and placed her down. As Bobby scanned the area for their next conquest, Roxy let out a loud yelp. Bobby looked down to see what ailed his partner, when Roxy yelped again, and stumbled to the ground. An object whistled past Bobby's legs and hit Roxy bouncing off the side of her body. The terrier was then hit a third time, and now yelped in pain continuously.

In a panic, Bobby looked towards the area where he thought the object came from, but saw nothing. He reached down, scooped up his faithful companion, scaled the wall, and made his way home as fast as he could. Bobby got home in tears and he and his mother rushed Roxy to the local animal hospital. Her yelps of pain became quieter during the short ride. By the time they arrived, Roxy was motionless in his arms. The veterinarian worked feverishly searching for a pulse on the animal. There was none to be found. The vet told them that blunt force trauma to the dog's vital organs caused massive internal bleeding leading to her death. Roxy died in Bobby's arms that day.

Despite his arrogance, Luther Vale never let it cloud his intelligence or cunning. Years ago, he solicited the help of a local attorney for his corporate aspirations. He held himself out as a security specialist and wanted to explore his options in a private capacity. Because he was already a police officer, Luther wanted to avoid the appearance of an impropriety. More importantly, he wanted to shield himself from any personal liability that could arise from the nature of his business. Based on these concerns, his attorney advised Luther to form a corporation to provide private security for his clients.

Naming the business was no easy task. It had to be authoritative and smart. It had to detail the man, and not just the business. After many weeks searching, he finally settled on the perfect name: *Acumen Holdings*. The dual jobs gave Luther, the eternal narcissist, the ultimate sense of power; a police officer by day and private security specialist when not in uniform. A rash of recent burglaries on Shelter Island caused a boom to his private practice. On this crisp morning in November 1972, Luther Vale of Acumen Holdings felt invigorated as he patrolled the grounds of the Rivington estate.

He had been longing to use his new high-powered pneumatic pellet gun, and when that little runt crossed onto the property with his mutt dog, it gave him the perfect opportunity to spring into action. Luther let out three shots to the dog, striking it broadside each time, and let out a hardy chuckle when the boy scrambled away with the mutt in his arms. That'll teach him a lesson he'll never forget, he proudly thought.

He then got a call on his two-way radio.

"Luther here" he said.

The voice asked, "Did you take care of it?"

"Affirmative," said Luther. "I hated to part with it though. That was my favorite truck. Hell, at least I can write it off as a business transaction. Over."

"Good," replied the voice in the radio.

After that exchange, Luther Vale never spoke of his Ford FT-735 Off Road Camper with anyone else again.

A few weeks later Bobby Manfredi entered a local store with some friends to buy some candy and soda pop. Luther Vale, in full uniform, walked in and spotted little Bobby.

He purchased some cigarettes and a coffee and before leaving, he leaned over to Bobby with a wicked smile before exiting, and said, "How's your dog?"

With those words, Bobby instantly knew that Luther shot Roxy. He desperately wanted to tell his parents, but was too afraid to do so. After all, who would believe a ten year old kid instead of a powerful police officer? Instead, Bobby left the store and never spoke of his encounter with Luther Vale, and his belief that he killed Roxy, to another soul.

# Comrade

I first met Andre Carter in law school and it was truly like meeting my spiritual twin. Similar life paths and experiences, created only through hard work and dedication, bind our kinship. Like me, Andre, or Dre as only his friends call him, was older than most of his peers and had to work full time while earning a legal education. Sharing the same bond has sealed our friendship, and a mutual understanding of life, that is as strong today as it was in law school.

After starting his post law-school career practicing corporate law, Dre eventually found his calling as a federal prosecutor. He is a no-nonsense, hard-nosed attorney whose strong life experience, full command of the law, and excellent trial skills have allowed him to rocket up the ranks in his department at the Eastern District of New York. The EDNY has wide jurisdiction in prosecuting federal crimes in New York, including Suffolk County, which encompasses the North Fork area.

Dre was keenly aware and staunchly supportive of my conviction, and I of his. He trusted me through and through in all matters, but when I called and asked him to meet me to discuss my research on the murder of a woman in the North Fork 37 years ago, he could not help but meet it with skepticism. We met outside of the Suffolk County Federal Court Building, a magnificent marble and glass structure in West Islip, New York.

"My man," Dre said with a wide smile as we shook hands.

We headed over to a local tavern for a late lunch.

We ordered some drinks and Dre asked, "Why do you care so

much about this case?"

"You know me, my friend," I replied. "What gets people like us so unhinged?"

"Injustice" he immediately retorted.

Smiling at the senselessness of asking a purely rhetorical question, I said, "Right, but not the ordinary plain vanilla injustice. It's a cruel world and bad things happen. People lie, people steal, or people lose their jobs at big law firms after they've staked all their hopes on it. No, I'm talking about a deeper level of injustice, the type where people use their power to suppress those who are subordinate to them. The type of injustice where the wicked murder the innocent in the middle of the night. That's real injustice, and it's a great motivator that cannot go unanswered by people like us who despise it so much. You know, Dre, I've always lived by the credo that when *you know you are right, then don't be afraid to push the envelope.* That is what I am doing here."

"I agree with you my brother," said Dre, "but in our line of work, to catch the bad guys, it's not what we know, it's what we can prove that counts."

"Dre," I replied, "this poor woman's life was snuffed out, and her body was tossed into a ditch in the middle of nowhere. At the time she was murdered she had an infant daughter, who, if still alive, probably never knew what happened to her mother. From what I have already seen, there are problems with the way this case was investigated. It seems to me that no one bothered to get to the bottom of this, like no one cared. Worst still, the killer was never found. That has to be made right."

Dre sipped his drink and said, "I don't see how I can help even if I wanted to. I work for a federal prosecutor and this sounds like a case where the local law enforcement has jurisdiction. Why don't you start with the local prosecutor's office?"

"Because I have reason to believe that state officials may be involved in covering up the crime," I replied. "The lead detective, who was making progress in the case, was removed by another detective who had a personal connection with a potential suspect. Isn't that a conflict there?"

Changing course, I said, "Let me ask you this Dre. Suppose a state crime was perpetrated by the local law enforcement, or local law enforcement was involved in a cover up, couldn't there be a federal civil rights violation?"

"Yes," he said.

"And wouldn't that give rise to federal jurisdiction?"

"Yes," he said again. "That's what we saw during the Civil Rights era."

I continued, "And to my knowledge, there is no statute of limitations on murder in New York, right?"

"Yes," he reiterated.

"Then, there it is," I retorted. "Your office could conceivably have jurisdiction to re-open the case and investigate what I have."

"That's a big leap of faith you make there," said Dre. "There has to be some violation of the United States Constitution for us to attain federal jurisdiction. For instance, we would have to show that excessive force was used by law enforcement against a person in a protected class like race or gender. Or, we could attain jurisdiction if there was a violation of the Commerce Clause. For instance, suppose there was a drug transaction where narcotics were carried across state lines. Or if a person was kidnapped in New York and brought to Pennsylvania. Those sorts of crimes would give us federal jurisdiction because they involve interstate commerce and/or crossing between at least two different states."

"So," I asked, "if there were grounds for federal jurisdiction, then your office could conceivably have the authority to reopen the case, right?"

When he nodded yes, I knocked exuberantly on the table and said "my man!"

We both ate burgers, ordered more drinks, and for the next hour, Dre listened as I explained the details of my findings. I informed him of my interview with lead reporter George McBride and our visit to the murder scene. I stressed how the only potential eyewitness account was omitted from the police report. I told him how I learned that Maria's daughter was only a few months old when Maria was killed, and of Ginny's account at how close Luther Vale was to the Rivington family, the same family whose son was rumored to have had an affair with the victim a year before she was murdered.

"That is all circumstantial," Dre said. "If you're talking about murder, you have to start by establishing motive. What motive do you have for this killing?"

"Well," I said, "The victim was employed at the Rivington's estate for several years and she was rumored to have had an affair with the only son of the Rivingtons. Then about a year later, she gives birth to a baby girl. A few months later, she is killed. It's likely that the young Rivington is the father of that baby. There could be a motive there."

Swirling the drink stirrer around in his glass, Dre said, "It all sounds fascinating for a romance novel. All kidding aside, that's not enough. There are too many breaks in the chain. There is nothing to indicate that the father even knew that the baby existed, and without that, there is no motive for him to kill her. Instead, a year goes by after she stops working for them, and then she dies. It could have been anyone who killed her. There is no viable connection to the Rivington boy."

I had no answer for my seasoned litigator friend. He was right. As it stands, motive cannot be established and the evidence is all circumstantial.

"Well," I said, "my next stop is upstate New York. I am going to visit the first detective to investigate the crime before he was removed from the case and then resigned. Maybe that will yield some new information."

"Upstate?" Dre asked with astonishment. "You really are passionate about this case, aren't you?"

I nodded in agreement.

"Look," he said, "establishing motive is the easiest of your worries. To open up a case this old, you need hard evidence like DNA or some other forensic evidence. We have a top of the line tech team and DNA has made leaps and bounds over the years, but this goes back to the 70's, so I don't know what, if any, hard evidence you can uncover. Even if you find some, there are many formidable challenges that a good defense attorney will make."

Sensing my dejection, he softened his stance.

"This is an election year, and my boss will not stick his ass out on the line and accuse some local officials for what looks like a circumstantial case at best. But if you can get some evidence and establish a reasonable motive, don't hesitate to call me. Otherwise, stay on the porch with the small dogs," he joked as he stood up and shook my hand before we parted ways.

Deflated, but by no means defeated, I thought long and hard at my next course of action. Evidence and motive are two elements that are clearly required to pry open such an old unsolved case. But I lacked any law enforcement authority, so how could I dig deeper into this case to attain the necessary pieces of the puzzle? Quitting was never my style, but Dre's pragmatic approach was raising great doubts within me. Still determined to carry on what I had started, leaving the tavern I knew then that my enthusiasm for this project would not soon be allayed. This quest for justice became the job that I lacked, a calling of some sorts, and as hard as it may be, the sound reasoning of my trusted colleague would not deter me from my purpose. Setting the GPS for upstate New York to pay a visit to John Conte, I wasn't quite sure what to expect, but if anyone could help fill the many gaps in this case, it certainly was him.

# In Search of a Better Life

The vast farms of the North Fork have always required a large pool of workers to yield their crops adequately for mass production. Beginning in the 1950's, migrant workers flocked to the area to fill this demand for labor. In an effort to accommodate the living quarters of these large groups of migrant workers, local farmers constructed so-called labor camps. These camps consisted of small barracks-style wooden cabins meant to house the workers and their children during the farming seasons. The cabins were filthy, overcrowded, and a natural fire hazard. Unfortunately, at these camps, workers were subjected to cruel treatment, unfair payment of wages, and manipulation designed to keep them mired in poverty and debt.

One of these camps existed in Cutchogue, New York. In 1960, a woman named Juana Cruz came to work and to reside here with her daughter Maria. Originally from Aguadilla, Puerto Rico, Juana left an abusive husband and dire poverty to settle in New York City. However, the scarce opportunities for work frustrated Juana who was strong and eager to work. Several of her friends informed Juana about the job opportunities on Long Island. Desperate to find stable employment so that she can provide a better life for her daughter, Juana and Maria relocated to the North Fork area to work the farms.

At first, a job was hard to come by. Most farmers ordinarily hired only African American workers and Juana was of Puerto Rican descent. Eventually, she was able to find work at a camp in Cutchogue. Ultimately, it was not that her race really mattered because in this harsh place, the only concern of the farmers, discriminatory or otherwise, was the ability of their workers to produce.

At the camps, Juana slaved away earning sub-par income and enduring harsh treatment from the farmers who reaped the benefits from her backbreaking work. Her daughter Maria was just ten years old at the time, and spent the long days in the company of the other children in the rickety sheds of the camp just waiting for a glimpse of her mother to return home from a grueling day of work in the hot sun. Each day, Juana would prepare breakfast and dinner for Maria, not fully understanding that the costs of each item consumed during such meals were deducted from her meager earnings and used to perpetuate the cycle of debt that she and so many like her were forever mired in.

Juana worked at the labor camp for nearly a decade. This took a tremendous toll on her body, and her health began to falter. Chronic back and joint pain was the norm, and even if proper medical treatment was accessible, it was certainly unaffordable. As Maria grew she longed to leave such a terrible place. She could not bear to see her mother continue to suffer, but Juana forbade Maria from working at the camp in her stead. When Maria turned 20, she joined some of the other camp children to search for work as laborers or domestic servants throughout the North Fork. The area had many "brokers" hired by wealthy families to procure suitable domestic workers for their estates. This method of seeking employment is naturally rife with its own peril, but Maria was desperate.

Maria's stunning natural beauty was only matched by her strong work ethic, and it wasn't long before she was noticed by several brokers, with one asking Maria if she would like to work at a family's estate on Shelter Island. Because the pay was good, the work promised to be steady, and most of all, it would enable her mother to stop working on the farms, Maria readily agreed. Having never been to Shelter Island, she asked the broker whom she would be working for, and she was told that it would be the Rivingtons.

# Pure Living in Hard Country

Deposit, New York is approximately 250 miles northwest of the North Fork region. The drive along Route 17 offers magnificent views of the Catskill Mountains. Prior to the opening of this highway, this drive took motorists though various small towns that boasted fine restaurants and shops. Now, with the highway bypassing these towns, most of these businesses were forced to close, leaving only the remnants of their prosperous past.

My GPS guided me off the highway and onto a state road that further cut through the mountains. While driving, I admired the various homes dotting the landscape. They ranged from large country style homes to smaller log cabins and trailers abutting large plots of land. There were vast cattle farms adorned with large barns, old tractors, and other farm equipment. The beautiful scenery was rife with reminders of the difficulties faced by living in such a remote area. There is no doubt about it. This was pure living in hard country. There were no other motorists on the road, so the few people that saw me driving by were cordial enough to give a friendly wave and a nod, and I reciprocated in kind. After turning onto a long gravel road, several deer spied my approach and scurried off the road into the thick pines.

Like many residents in the area, John Conte lived in a trailer that sits just off the gravel road. To the rear is a magnificent view of his property, which boasts a large pond in the middle of a vast open field. As I exited my car, a beaver spotted my approach and quietly slipped back into the pond for cover. The field beyond spanned at least 300 yards and had large bales of hay that were strewn about, likely to be shipped to local farmers to feed their cattle. Electrical power lines dotted the rear of the field, and beyond them lay a thickening forest of large pine trees.

My approach was greeted by loud bangs from tools being used and a few obscenities uttered by a man working underneath the rear of the trailer. I could see a pair of faded jeans and white sneakers protruding from underneath.

"John Conte?" I asked aloud.

"Yeah," he answered hastily. "Who is it?"

"Savoy Graves. We spoke yesterday. I told you I was coming to ask you a few questions about your time spent on the police force."

"Hand me that wrench, will ya?" he asked.

I happily obliged.

After a few minor adjustments, Conte slid out from under the trailer, stood up to wipe his hands on his oversized flannel shirt, and put out his hand to shake mine. At well over six feet tall, he was a hulking figure with broad shoulders and hands that were the size of oven mitts. He appears to be in his early sixties, but despite his age, he was fitter than many men that are half his age. Not necessarily fit in the athletic sense, but instead more of the true workhorse type.

"Come on in Mr. Graves," he said as he stepped into the trailer.

I followed him into the fairly small living space. On his table to the right lay large milk crates containing everything from tools to food product. To the left and past the small kitchen, were two small bedrooms and a bathroom to the rear. Space was clearly at a premium, but Mr. Conte uses all of it wisely.

"Please excuse the mess. I have been busy making repairs to get ready for next winter. It's never too soon to prepare," he said.

"No worries," I said. "Now seems like the best time to do it. How long have you been living up here?"

"Oh, it must be nearing 40 years," he replied. "I bought the trailer and the land from an old German family. Nice people. It's a bit rough up here at times, with the weather and all, but I like it."

"Mr. Conte, I would like to ask you about your experience as a police officer."

"Please call me John," he said. "I spent a great deal of time on the force, Mr. Graves, can you be more specific?"

"Sure," I said. "Sorry about that, it was a long drive."

He offered me a cold bottle of water as we sat down at the table.

After taking a long drink of water, I asked him if he would share some of his experiences while working on the police force in the North Fork.

"Oh yes," he replied. "That was a dream job compared to some of the other areas I worked in New York. I left in 1973. I took my pension and hit the road. I was tired of police work so I came up here to hunt, fish, and just live off the land."

"I can understand that," I said as I looked out the window to admire the beauty.

"Honestly," he continued. "I got tired of police work."

Then, catching himself, he said, "Why exactly are you here Mr. Graves?"

"Well," I replied, "I am an attorney currently in between jobs. I stumbled onto a news story about the death of a woman named Maria Cruz. She…"

He immediately interrupted and said, "Mr. Graves, I have a lot of work to catch up on around here. Everything I know about that matter is in the police report. I don't know how I can be of assistance."

Then he stood up to shake my hand and pushed open the trailer door for me to leave.

Refusing to be deterred, I continued.

"John, I drove a long way to get here. I may be chasing a ghost, but I believe there is more to Maria's death than what's in the reports. Can you please spare a few more minutes of your time?"

He smiled and said, "Sure, but let's take a walk. I need some fresh air."

We exited the trailer, crossed the gravel road, and began to walk up a steep hill littered with "*No Trespassing*" signs. The road climbed up on a modest incline before levelling off.

"This here is an old rock quarry," John said. "I should have bought this land when I had the chance. The neighbors beat me to it by only a few months. They turned around and sold it to a company that produces rock and slate for companies like Home Depot and Lowe's. The lucky bastard made millions and now lives somewhere in Florida. They've gotten most of the rock out of here so the quarry is pretty much deserted."

I studied the area with amazement. It was strewn with old discarded items. Tools, tractor equipment, old work helmets, and littered garbage served as remnants of a busy past. We neared the edge of the pit, peering down over the rock quarry, which must have been at least two hundred feet deep. As I focused on the jagged rock on the bottom, John grabbed me with his oversized paws, nudged me close to the edge, and held me firmly.

"Mr. Graves," he said, "this is a terrible place for an accident to happen. Wouldn't you agree?"

I nodded in fear as he continued.

"So tell me, why are you here and who are you working for?"

I repeated my story regarding research into Maria's death.

"Who are you working for?" he barked again.

"No one," I said.

He nudged me closer to the precipice.

I drew a breath.

"Maria's daughter, Lola…Lola Cruz. I am working for Lola Cruz."

With a puzzled look, he whispered, "Impossible," as he pulled me slightly back from the edge, softening his grip as he looked away.

"You're shitting me, she had a daughter?" he asked.

"Yes" I replied. "I am not really working as her attorney, but I am just trying to uncover the truth about her mother's murder and the identity of her father. Once I have enough, I will be contacting her, or at least hope to contact her. You see, I heard the rumor of Maggie Taves' eyewitness testimony that never made it into the report. I know about Luther Vale's close connection to the Rivingtons. And I know that you were making serious progress until you were removed from the case. I am here to find out why, and any other information you can provide to me.

Now that we've cleared that up," I said nervously looking down into the pit, "can we talk, and I mean really talk?"

With his left hand still firmly clutching my shirt, John pulled me back to a safe distance from the edge and asked, "Do you know where she is?"

"I have an address," I responded "but have not tried to contact her yet until I have some more information. I mean, why open a can of worms?" I asked meekly.

"She deserved a better fate," John said. "And so did her mother."

Taking a cigarette out of his top pocket, he lit it and took a deep drag.

"I believe you Mr. Graves," he said. "Maybe it's time for justice. Hell, at my age, what have I got to lose?"

"Come on, follow me," he added. "I will tell you everything I know. Hey, no hard feelings there, huh? I didn't know if I could trust you."

I nodded yes, as we headed back down the winding trail, across the road and into the trailer. It was clear that John's head was swirling with thought on this matter, and I smiled sensing another wheel of justice begin to crank into motion. I also knew that I needed a drink to calm my hands that were shaking, since just a few minutes ago I was nearly tossed to my death at the bottom of an abandoned rock quarry.

# Desire

The two lovers have made it a regular practice to sneak off and satisfy each other's desire wherever they could. On that warm summer night, it would be no different. They met by the pool, and quietly slipped off to the beach. As they strolled, he sighed. The typical ploy of a young man craving attention. She held his hand and asked what is wrong. He lamented at the very different worlds in which they each resided laden with rules that kept them apart. He longed to walk freely with her and to have their love accepted.

Gently raising his chin, she kissed him softly on the cheek. As she retreated, he asked if he could kiss her. She paused, and with a sweet smile, leaned in to accept his offer. Her touch was gentle, but her passion was fierce. Consumed with an irresistible force, the two kissed passionately. With the world ceasing to exist around them, they stumbled onto the sand feverishly undressing each other as they kissed.

Fully unclothed, he laid on top of her. She enjoyed the full force of his weight. He slowly slid down offering gentle kisses to her breasts, stomach, and thighs until he spread her legs and reached her warm moist folds, which he eagerly explored with his tongue, lips, and fingers. Her thighs clenched tightly over his ears as her hands held the back of his head firmly in place. Intoxicated by her taste, he increased his pace until her legs shook violently from a powerful orgasm. He then rose, pleased by the effects of his efforts, and positioned himself to enter her. She wrapped her long legs around his back guiding him into her, and let out a sweet groan when he complied. He moved in and out of her as the two kissed feverishly. Her hands were placed firmly on his buttocks, forcing him into her deeper with each thrust. He tried to slow his pace so as to forestall his climax, but her gyrating hips and squeezing warmth would have none of that. His pace instead quickened, his body tensed, and without a thought or desire of ever stopping, he released inside of her. She shuddered with delight, pulling him in even tighter.

He fell off to the side of her as the two lay breathless looking at the stars and listening to the waves. She wrapped her leg over his, placing her soft hand on his chest to feel his rapidly beating heart. The two lay speechless with only the sea and the sky to have witnessed their unbridled passion. It was a night of pleasure that neither of them have ever known in their young lives. It was primal, it was powerful, and it was love.

But, unbeknownst to them, there was another witness to this consummation. Rosemary Rivington watched in horror from the nearby dune as her brother Chet and Maria Cruz violated the sacred rule of the Rivington household.

# A Cross to Bear

Still unsettled from my near death encounter, I sipped from a glass of scotch that John had poured for me before he retreated to the rear of the trailer to dig up his files. He returned with yet another large milk crate containing several folders, which he set on the table.

Before removing any of the contents, he said "What I am about to tell you has not been shared with another soul for over 30 years."

I listened intently.

"I was on the Southold Police force for about two years. The area was great. Nice towns, with real nice people. Any action we had was usually during the summer months. You know, DWI busts, fights in the bar, and stuff like that. It was in early October of 1972. The summer season was over, and things really started to quiet down. I was finishing up a nice breakfast before going out on patrol when a call came in over the radio. Dispatch said something was found in an open field over in Orient. So I took a ride over. Some local kids were playing in field about 200 yards off the road and complained of a foul odor. They told their parents, who called it in. I was the first officer on the scene. I approached the area, got down on my knees, and removed some dirt to reveal what I already knew it would be. Once you come across a dead body, you never forget that smell. It was a decomposing female body partially wrapped in plastic."

John began to remove some folders from the milk crate and placed them carefully onto the table. I poured over the items with great intrigue. The files contained crime scene photos, the coroner's report, testimony from potential witnesses, and personal hand-written notes.

"Those are my notes," he clarified.

I spent a great deal of time looking at the crime scene photos. They were horrific. There in the pristine field lay the dead body of Maria Cruz. Her hair was long and frayed. Her once beautiful face was shattered by a mauled nose and broken teeth. Her eyes remained open in a cold stare. Her hands were badly bruised as well, with several fingernails broken off, probably from a vain attempt to resist being dragged further into the field. Maria was still in her brown work uniform, similar to those I've seen worn by employees of the Oyster Cove Inn. Even though the powder blue patch on the uniform was partially torn, I could make out the lower half of the mermaid inside a seashell.

She was last seen alive on the night of September 23, 1972, and the autopsy estimates the date of death on or about that date. The official cause of death is multiple stab wounds to her heart, although it appears that one would have done the deed. There were no signs of sexual assault, just the brutal and apparently hateful act of violence. I read on intently as John sipped his drink and gazed out the window overlooking the pond.

Breaking the silence, John said, "It's pretty bad, I know. But it's what's not in the report that really raises eyebrows."

John pulled out a second folder from the milk crate.

"This folder," he said, "has my own findings, both from the initial investigation and from what I found after being removed from the case."

The file was in meticulous order. I studied the documents carefully.

The first item of interest was a set of notes from John's interview with Maggie Taves.

"She was rambling," he said, "but to be honest, I believed her. She insisted, to me anyway, that there was a vehicle in the area that night. An orange and white flatbed truck. When Luther took over the case, he disregarded Maggie's testimony as coming from an unreliable source."

"I spoke to George McBride yesterday," I interrupted, "the local newspaper reporter at the time. He told me that Maggie suffered from a mental illness. Unfortunately, she died last year."

"That's sad," replied John. "She definitely had an illness, but her account was coherent, almost as if she saw more, but was unwilling to tell it. It was easy for Luther to dismiss her as a crazy old bat, but in my experience, where there's smoke, there's fire. I'm convinced that Maggie saw something."

I nodded in agreement, as John continued.

"Anyway, I wanted to follow up on this lead further, I tried to speak with Maggie afterwards, but she refused to talk to me again. I never understood why. That's when I started to notice a shift against me. I became more and more marginalized on the force. I was purposely kept away from the investigation."

"Privately," he said, "I kept looking into the case. The field where Maria was dragged across was loaded with forensic evidence that could have helped us track down the killer. DNA science wasn't as strong then as it is now, but blood and hair samples were still heavily reliable. Surely the killer had to struggle to drag Maria through the field, and that must have left blood, teeth, nails, and hair. Even the direction in which she was dragged could have yielded important clues. And there were tire tracks from a car near where the body was found."

Intrigued, I looked through the report to find this information.

"You won't find that in any of the reports," said John. "A forensics team was slow in getting to the crime scene, and by the next day a local farmer named Thorne plowed the field clean. He claimed that that he was told to do so by Luther Vale. Vale denied it, threatening to bring the farmer up on charges for tampering with evidence, but that never happened. They chalked it up to a 'misunderstanding'. The way I saw it, that was negligence at best on Vale's part. Maybe even criminal negligence."

"It took us over a week just to identify Maria's body. A missing person's call came in from the Oyster Cove Inn, and we found Maria's car there. We matched prints found in her car to the body, and her boss confirmed Maria's identity from photographs of her. Other than learning her identity, we found nothing else. No family or next of kin. Just a dead girl."

"Do you know what happened to her body?" I asked.

"I heard that it was sent over to Potter's Field on Hart Island. That's where they sent all the bodies that are unclaimed. They bury them in mass graves. You'll never find her in that mess."

"Did you speak with Laura about anything else?" I asked.

"No," he replied. "We were too busy running the prints and getting whatever evidence we could from the car. I planned to go back and interview all of Maria's coworkers, but that never happened. Vale had taken over the investigation by then."

I looked at a picture of Ginny Foster in the file.

"That's Virginia Foster," he said. "She was the cook at the Rivington's estate. I never had the chance to talk to her."

"She told me that Luther Vale interviewed her," I said.

"I can't understand how they would have allowed that," replied John. "Luther Vale did some private security work for the Rivingtons. It was the worst kept secret in the North Fork.

"The only lead we had was that Maria used to work at the Rivington estate. There were rumors that she had an affair with the young son before she left, which was about a year before her death. Before I had a chance to interview Chet, I spoke with his father Winston Rivington. He was a very standoffish son of a bitch, and didn't show an ounce of remorse for Maria's death. Hoping to push him for some information, I asked about the rumored affair. His face got red and he told me to leave at once. Two weeks later, I was thrown off the case. A few months after that I left the force completely. I've been up here ever since."

"John," I said, "I have to ask. What made you retire from the force instead of just transferring? I mean, you said it was a dream job."

John peered out the window glassy eyed. I regretted asking a question that obviously evokes such a painful memory and was about to apologize when he decided to speak.

"Before I joined the Southold Police Force, I was a beat cop patrolling the streets of Cypress Hills, New York. I was known by the local citizens as a tough, but fair cop. To the vandals, and there were many, I was known as a hard ass. I used to carry this over-sized flashlight that had the weight of a lead pipe. I called it *'The Persuader.'* When perps got out of hand, I would give them a quick jab with it, and they quickly fell into line. At that time, many cops had their own tools like a billy-club, or the butt of their gun. For me it was my flashlight.

"There was this schoolyard where the local kids often hung out. They would have giant parties in the back of the poorly lit schoolyard where they would put kegs of beer inside garbage cans. Sons of bitches thought they were invisible. But they were mostly harmless. A group of kids from the neighborhood acting out their drunk teenage fantasies, singing to the anthems of the time, like *"Baba O'Riley"* by the Who, where *"Teenage Wasteland"* was their slogan. Anyway, we usually let them have their fun on the weekends until midnight when we would break it up. It was funny. We would rush in sending the crowd scrambling in all directions. If we were in the mood and there was enough beer left, we'd haul some of it back to the precinct for the boys to have a few drinks.

"There was hardly any serious trouble until that one fateful night. My partner and I got a call over the radio about a disturbance in the schoolyard. It was a cold night, and the usual suspects were there with bottles of brandy instead of the usual beer kegs. They lit a makeshift fire in a metal garbage can and poked holes in it. We thought it was the usual, you know disorderly conduct, pissing in public and the like. But that night, there was a larger group than usual. A rival group of kids had come from another neighborhood looking for trouble.

"Among the crowd was the local ring leader, Lenny Plevoras, or 'Lenny Plev,' as he was known to his buddies. Lenny was a tough kid, in and out of both school and jail, and for some reason the rest of the group looked up to him. When we got there, Lenny and some other kid were pounding the shit out of each other in the middle of a large crowd that cheered them on. Armed with the Persuader, I went in to break it up. Lenny swung wildly towards the face of this kid. His fist missed its mark, and instead caught me right in the jaw. Solid shot by that little fucker. The kid on the bottom scrambled away, leaving me and Lenny to square off. These kids normally act tough, especially in front of their crew, but none of them were ever stupid enough to go toe-to-toe with the cops. But Lenny had this look in his eye, you know, like there was no going back.

"Instead of retreating, Lenny charged and placed his shoulder into my gut forcing me back. I kept my balance, lifted him by his chest, and flung him to the side. There was no way he was coming back for more, or so I thought. He charged again, this time flailing a wild right hand catching me in the nose. Before he could retreat, I caught him good with my flashlight, right to the side of his head and neck. He scrambled two steps back and dropped like a stone.

"My partner quickly scrambled over to cuff Lenny as I wiped the blood that was pouring out of my nose. Then I heard a girl scream and people started making a loud commotion. As I turned back, I saw my partner leaning over Lenny Plev, who was on his back convulsing profusely. My partner looked at me with astonishment and shook his head. I called for backup. More kids screamed and some cried as Lenny was flopping on the floor like a fish out of water before going unconscious. Within minutes, the schoolyard was swarming with police and ambulance personnel.

"Lenny Plev spent six months in the hospital. He suffered partial brain damage from the blow to the head that would leave him with slurred speech for the rest of his life. Not a day goes by that

I don't stop to think about that poor kid. Even though I knew I wasn't wrong, the stars were lining up against me very quickly, and I was being investigated for police brutality. Witnesses claimed that I engaged Lenny as a ploy just to use excessive force with my flashlight that they said I often wielded with impunity. Both my partner and I testified that I acted in self-defense, but once the press got wind of the story, all hell broke loose. The neighborhood was in an uproar and the brass wasn't pleased. For the first time in my career, I was scared.

"To calm the greater public, I was placed on desk duty, and that was the beginning of the end. With me facing all types of charges, my union rep urged me to resign. She knew of an open position out in Southold, and all parties agreed that was my best and only way out. It was hard to leave the streets I've known and loved for all those years for the desolate countryside of the North Fork, but I really had no choice. I was too young to retire, and too much of a cop to leave police work.

"I thought my story would be kept quiet, but word leaked out, and once Luther Vale learned of it, I knew that he would not hesitate to use it against me. I guess I intimidated him or something. So, from the minute I joined the new force, I was on a tight leash, and anytime there was a potential run-in with a perp or difficult crime scene, it made me hesitate, and this affected my police work. In Maria's case, once I started asking too many questions to the wrong people, I was doomed.

"A week before leaving the force, I was in the locker room changing for my shift when Luther walked in. He already knew about my interview with Maggie Taves and Winston Rivington, and he wasn't happy about it. But what really ticked him off were my complaints about the field being plowed clean. He was bitching about me sticking my nose where it didn't belong.

"Never one to back down, I went nose to nose with him and said, 'How the hell does an active crime scene get swept clean? Either you fucked up by accident or on purpose.'

"He smirked, trying to be the big man that he thought he was, and said, 'Fucked up? You mean like you did with Lenny Plev. That's right. Everyone around here knows how you attacked that poor kid. It takes a real tough guy to do that.'

"Without hesitation, I punched him right in the jaw. He flew back into some lockers and regained his balance, but before we could engage, some officers jumped in to break it up.

"'You did it now, big man,' he kept saying. 'You did it now.'

"Of course he brought me up on charges, and instead of heading into their kangaroo court, and without any other real option, I resigned. I took my pension and left."

"Any regrets," I asked.

"Just one," he said. "That I didn't get to finish kicking his ass. Let me warn you though. Vale is a dangerous man. I don't know if he is still alive, but if he is, you better stay clear of him. If he was involved in Maria's murder, he would do anything to keep it a secret."

John stood up and went to the sink to wipe his face with some water as I thought about his admonition regarding Luther. Given everything I've heard in this case, it seemed wise to stay clear of him. Now with Conte's warning, I knew that it was the best thing to do. Then my attention focused back to the milk crate. I saw an envelope with a small velvet bag inside. I opened it to find a silver chain adorned with a plain silver cross. It had some dirt on it, but otherwise was in excellent condition.

John returned to the table and said, "That was found around Maria's neck. The coroner gave it to me, and it somehow got placed in my file."

I handed it to him as he looked at it intently for a moment.

Then he reached to give it back to me and said, "Do me a favor, will you? If you find Maria's daughter, give this to her. The poor girl should have something of her mother's. And tell her I am sorry that I couldn't do more to solve the crime."

I thanked John for the hospitality and the information he has shared with me.

As I stood to leave, I asked, "John, if need be, will you come back to testify to your knowledge of the case?"

He looked out the trailer window long and hard. Two ducks had just landed on the pond causing slight ripples in the otherwise serene water.

After taking a moment to reflect, he said, "Damn straight I will."

I smiled, thanked him again, and left the trailer.

# Vestige

Lola stood before Lita's grave in the small cemetery in Queens, New York. She visits this serene place as often as she can, and when she does, she brings two bouquets of flowers. One is for Lita, who shares the grave with two other distant relatives. The other bouquet is for her mother. Such a ritual takes on a particular sadness for two reasons. The first, and most obvious, is because this unknown woman brought her into this world. And every day Lola is alive, she gives thanks to her for that.

The other less observable reason for this sad ritual is that Lola has no other place in which to express sympathies for her deceased mother. Thus, Lola has been cruelly denied both the opportunity to have known her mother, and to have an adequate place in which she can mourn her. For a young Catholic woman, this was especially challenging.

On this cloudy day, under God's watchful eye, Lola Cruz paid respects to Lita, the only vestige of a parent she has ever known, and respects to the phantom mother she never knew. She looked at the sky in search of answers, of a sign, of anything, but other than a passing train from the elevated station across the street from the cemetery, there were no signs bestowed upon her that day.

# Moonlight

I arrived back in the North Fork area just past seven o'clock and picked up a sandwich, some drinks, and a cup of coffee, which gave me the much-needed energy to continue my research. Instead of returning to my cottage at the Oyster Cove, my plan was to go back to Orient to visit the site of the murder. The Farmer's Almanac reported a full moon on September 23, 1972, the night the murder was said to have occurred. With an expected full moon tonight, I wanted to wait in the field until nightfall and take in the scenery. This seemed to be the best way to recreate the setting from the night of the murder.

I sat under the tree and began eating the sandwich while reflecting on poor Maria. The area is so desolate that if she was able to scream, she would have never been heard out here. And at night, no one would have seen a thing. With dusk settling in, the field was even more serene than before. Everything just seemed to stop. Even the nesting ospreys were silent, and except for the gentle waves from the bay, there was absolute silence. As the sun began to set, my body finally succumbed to sleep.

I awoke a short while later with nightfall completely arrived. If not for the full moon, which illuminated the entire field, I would not be able to see my hand in front of my face. Since there was a full moon on the night of the murder, it is conceivable that a passerby in the area could have seen the grisly act taking place. From my seated position, I scanned the area slowly from left to right. Most of the homes had a partially obstructed view. The one with the best view, however, was Maggie's house, but it's too far to have offered a clear view, even if Maggie had binoculars.

There were several other homes, but none of them offer a better view of this location. Glancing back in the other direction, lights in Maggie's house and movement from the first floor window caught my eye. I called George McBride to ask, and to his knowledge, no one has lived in Maggie's house since her death.

"It could be her son Hatcher," he said. "Someone told me yesterday that she saw him in town earlier this week."

I thanked George, gathered my things, and made the slow walk back to the car. The sound of a car door closing near Maggie's house caught my attention. It was a man searching for something in his car. Seizing the moment, I walked over, introduced myself, and told him about the nature of my research. Sure enough, it was Maggie's son Hatcher and he was more than happy to talk to me.

"Mr. Taves, I met with George McBride yesterday and he told me about your mother. Do you have a few minutes to talk?"

"Sure," he replied. "I remember George. He was very close to my mom. Let's go inside."

Hatcher Taves is a tanned, middle aged, stout fellow with a receding hairline. His reddened eyes were a clear sign that he was still mourning the death of his mother. We sat in the living room as he told me stories of his family. The home was decorated with outdated furniture, numerous framed pictures hanging from the walls, and bad wallpaper. The smell of bleach permeated the air, presumably to remove the smell of Maggie's decomposed body once it was found.

"Everyone around here thought she was crazy as bat shit," said Hatcher recapturing my attention. "There was no doubt that she had a serious mental illness, but she dealt with her issues. My mother was a smart, capable, and loving woman," he said sadly, "and I like to think that she lived a good life until her death last year. It took me a while to get out here to handle the affairs of her estate, but now that I am here, it is no less easy dealing with her death."

I expressed my condolences.

"Mr. Taves, I am retracing the Maria Cruz case." I continued. "I spoke with the first officer assigned to the investigation, John Conte. He told me that your mother may have been a witness to the crime, but her statements were never admitted into the final report."

"Oh," Hatcher replied, "My mother never said anything to me about it, but to be honest, she was widely known to have 'seen' things in the night. No one ever took her too seriously."

I asked if he was aware of anything that she may have left behind that could yield some clues, like a journal or pictures.

"Well," he replied, "You are more than free to look around. She kept a lot of her old stuff in the attic."

Hatcher stood up, walked over to a hallway outside a bedroom, and pulled the chain lowering the steps to the attic. He cautioned about the rickety steps as I prepared to ascend.

"If you need any help, just give me a yell," he said, "I have some important paperwork to go over."

I thanked him as I slowly headed up the stairs and turned on the lights.

My ascension into the attic was immediately met with the smell of a bad combination of mothballs, cat urine, and cedar. There was dust and spider webs everywhere. I treaded carefully, shifting my weight only onto the most stable planks of plywood strewn about the floor. The entire space was a hopeless wreck of random antiques, old furniture, and scattered boxes.

I moved slowly toward the front of the attic, facing an old paned window overlooking the front of the house. It must offer a spectacular view in the daylight, I thought, as I peered out the window. An old exhaust fan lay disconnected next to the window, which explained the rancid smell. I scanned the area, and in the darkened corner, there were several cardboard boxes. I noticed one particular box partially sealed with duct tape. An electrical cord was protruding from the top corner of the box, and the tape, which appeared to have lost much of its adhesiveness in the humid space, was dangling over the side.

Hoping to get a view of its contents, I tugged slightly at the tape on the top of the box, which put up more of a fight than I imagined, and inside saw what appeared to be some type of a home recording device, several encased reels of film, and Polaroid pictures. The pictures were taken from a great distance and all of the same place: a long open field. Each of the pictures had arrows, coordinates, and other random markings made with red ink pointing to a specific location in the field, which looked somewhat similar to the site where Maria's body was found. The osprey aerie was absent, and the four adjacent trees were much smaller, but the background with the shimmering water of Hallock's Bay is the same. I peered out the window again, and with the moonlight, it seemed as if the pictures were taken from this location. I returned to the other pictures as a spider scurried across the top of the box, momentarily breaking my attention. Flicking it off, I continued to review the other items in the box.

I carefully removed the home recorder, which despite the accumulation of dust on the device, appeared to be in good condition. It reminded me of an old super 8-millimeter recorder that my parents used to have when I was young. The recording device was fitted with a long scope attached to its side. This also seemed to be in good shape. I carefully replaced the recorder in the box and studied the smaller boxes inside which housed reels of film.

Checking the titles of each reel, I found most were random home movies and other family engagements from the Taves' family. Hatcher would enjoy these, I thought. One reel that caught my eye was entitled *"Full Moon, 9/72."* Since the farmer's almanac reported a full moon on the night of the murder in 1972, I wondered if this film could somehow be related to the murder. Exploding with anxiety, I put all the items back in the box, and rushed down the attic stairs as fast as I could.

I called out to Hatcher who was sitting at the kitchen table reviewing some documents.

"Have you seen this box before?" I asked.

"No" he said as he began to empty its contents onto the table.

"I do remember this recorder though," he said proudly. "My dad got it when I was young. It was way ahead of its time and quite innovative.

See this scope?" he asked. "It's called a Starlight Scope. It was used in the Vietnam War for night combat. One of the many mementos my dad took from the war. My dad was a camera enthusiast. He always played around with this kind of stuff. With this, he used a special adaptor to affix the night vision scope onto the home recorder and, just like that, he was able to record video at night."

Here, look through the lens," he asked as he shut the lights off and held the camera towards the window.

I was amazed at the clear night vision it produced.

"Like I said," he replied, "way ahead of its time."

I asked why his father would have a need for night vision.

"My dad spent a lot of time in the war fighting at night. He got used to being out in the dark. Once he met my mom, they would often go on nature walks past sunset and record the surroundings at night. It brought them peace," he said.

"Did your mother still do this after your father died?" I asked.

"Probably," he said proudly. "She enjoyed it too. Like I said, she wasn't always crazy."

Careful not to let him know how far I've pried, I held out the reel box marked *"Full Moon: 9/72"* and asked if it was a home movie.

"It doesn't ring a bell," he said.

"Do you mind if we take a look?" I asked.

"No, of course not. Let me find the screen" he said as he climbed into the attic and quickly descended with it.

He arranged the projector on the edge of the table, plugged it in, adjusted the screen a few feet away, and said, "Hit the lights."

Although its images were green and a bit grainy, the bright light of the moon and the makeshift night vision device produced surprisingly good footage. The film opens with a view of a vast open field in bright moonlight. The person appears to be walking slowly in the film with minimal shaking, a sign of an experienced user, I thought. Moments later, the angle of the film quickly adjusts downward as it appears that the person crouched down. Seconds after that, the angle of the film adjusts to capture a large figure dragging what appears to be another person across the field by the hair. The distance between the person filming and the brute could not have been more than thirty yards. A few minutes later, the figure appears to strike the victim while forcing the body down to the ground. Seconds later, an unidentifiable car appears from the right, kicking up dust from the field. A person much smaller than the other figure, but too far to ascertain the identity, exits from the driver's side of the vehicle.

Then, with full clarity that only the brilliant moon and primitive night vision equipment could provide, the large figure holds up what appears to be a knife, and, as if in some ritualistic orgy of violence, drives it down once…twice…a third time…into the victim's chest. The camera shakes violently for a moment, likely from fear in the person filming the macabre images, but not enough to deviate entirely from the scene. The victim lay motionless as the second person re-enters the vehicle and drives off. After a short pause, the brute rolls the body into a ditch, picks up a shovel, and begins to cover the body with the dirt stacked nearby.

The camera slowly pans back from the scene as if the person filming is moving backwards, but always keeping the fiend in sight as he is burying the body. Minutes go by before a vehicle can be seen parked on the road at the end of the field. At all times the killer can still be seen in the background continuing the sinister duty of burying the body. The film then zooms in to the vehicle, which appears to be a pickup truck, and centers in on the license plate, which is marked *ESE9793*. Then the film abruptly cuts off.

My eyes remained glued onto the screen for a few more seconds, half expecting more footage, but there was none.

My hands were now shaking. Judging by the date on the reel, and the all-too-familiar location of the murder, Hatcher and I had just witnessed the murder of Maria Cruz. The callous disregard for human life was sickening and I nearly vomited. Regaining my composure, I struggled to understand why this evidence wasn't produced. Even if no one would have believed Maggie's oral testimony, this film would have proved her account to everyone.

Still stunned, I cleared my throat, and turned to Hatcher.

"As I told you, I have a friend who is an attorney that works as a federal prosecutor. He is aware of my research and said that he can only help if I can produce hard evidence. I think we can both agree that we have just seen some hard evidence. With your permission, I would like to take this film to him. Would you allow me to?"

"Hold on a minute here," Hatcher replied. "Let me think this through. Shouldn't this go to the police?"

"Hatcher," I replied, "under normal circumstances I would say yes, but these aren't normal circumstances. I can't be certain, but there is a possibility that local law enforcement may have been involved in covering up this crime. Besides, my friend is a federal prosecutor. Once I get it to him, he can best decide how to proceed."

He paused for a moment and said, "All those local bastards always thought that my mother was crazy. Even the cops too. My mother used to tell me how bad they used to treat her. Yes, you can bring it to him, but on one condition. If you catch the bastards who did this, you make sure that you tell them that it was Maggie Taves who caught them. And that she wasn't so crazy after all."

I agreed, shaking his hand before packing up the equipment into the box, and exiting the home. As I started the car, all I could think about were Dre's words: "hard evidence."

# Heavy Burden

I got back to my cottage with my hands still shaking. Witnessing the murder of another human being is something that will remain with me for the rest of my life. Unlike a Hollywood movie, where one can compartmentalize such images as entertainment, this was real, and far more shocking. It was an utter disregard for human life exhibited by a killer who murdered another human being before burying the body as casually as throwing out trash.

My mind shifted back to the filming of the truck. In focusing in on the license plate, it was clear that the person who shot the film was trying to offer a lead on the killer's identity. If the registrant of the truck could be found, then so too could the killer's identity. But that was 37 years ago. It's highly unlikely that the vehicle is still in one piece, let alone in the New York area.

While working at Powell & Mason, a colleague of mine during preparation for trial, excelled in the filing of requests under the Freedom of Information Law, or FOIL request, to ascertain governmental information. Since all vehicles in New York State had to be registered with the Department of Motor Vehicles, then such information should be obtainable. I perused through the DMV website for information requests, pleased to learn that these types of requests can now be satisfied much quicker, and in some cases within five business days.

The online application for a DMV FOIL request lists a variety of credentials required to make such requests, most of which did not apply to my research. However, one option included:

*"Research activities and for use in providing statistical details, so long as the personal information is not published or used to contact individuals."*

That was the only option similar to my search, so I checked it, completed the rest of the application, and paid the small fee to complete the online request.

New fears began to creep into my mind. To my knowledge, the only people who have ever seen this footage are myself, Hatcher, and the deceased Maggie. Now being in possession of this evidence evoked a crushing sense of responsibility to ensure that it gets into the right hands. Every impulse in my body told me to bring it immediately to Dre to show it to him. But it was late at night, so it would have to wait until tomorrow. I texted Dre to tell him of my need to visit him in the morning. He responded, telling me to meet him at 9:30.

A hot shower did little to help me relax. My mind was racing. I kept peering out the window toward my car, worried about the film that was currently stored in the trunk. Could anyone know that it was in my possession? Or was paranoia just setting in? After an hour of restlessness, I got out of bed and went to the car to retrieve the entire bag. It was too important to leave to chance, even if I was just being paranoid. With the film now packed neatly under my bed, and the door locked with a chair propped up against the doorknob for extra security, my nervousness waned enough to allow me finally to get some sleep.

# A Patriarch Lost

On the morning of February 17, 2005, after visiting a friend, Winston Rivington was in his car returning to his home on Shelter Island. He was motoring down the scenic Route 25 near Orient when he felt a crushing pain in his chest. He struggled to maintain control, but lost consciousness as his car veered off the road crashing into a shallow ditch. The official cause of death was a massive heart attack.

In his will, and much to his wife's consternation, Winston requested that, upon his death, his body shall be cremated, with his ashes dispersed in Gardiner's Bay in a small ceremony. Although Sarah would see to it that his wishes were granted, she first demanded an elaborate funeral service to take place at their home. Hundreds of mourners came to Shelter Island to pay their respects. In a rare showing of respect by a public service to a private individual, the ferry service from both the north and south forks were closed to the public for several hours, only providing shuttles to those attending the funeral. Only a Rivington could command such respect.

Sarah Rivington stood silently near the coffin, mourning the loss of her beloved husband. She was dressed in an elegant black Chanel suit with her hair pulled back in a bun. She wore dark sunglasses to mask her pain. Her children stood by her side, awkwardly trying to comfort their grieving mother. For the Rivingtons, this was just another façade aimed at outwardly confirming the belief that they were a tightknit family. The pretentious world in which they lived demanded such a spectacle, a fact that was not lost upon anyone in attendance.

After the service, Sarah, Chet, and Rosemary boarded their yacht with a priest and a few close family members and friends. The vessel set off into Gardiner's Bay. After a short ride and a few spoken words by each family member, Winston's remains were ceremoniously scattered over the bay. Sarah watched silently mired in thought that, for the first time since she married her beloved husband, she was now alone. The children also had time to reflect on their loss, but given the frail health of their mother, their thoughts were far less sorrowful, and instead were more focused on the fate of the family fortune.

# Hit the Lights

Dre's office was not what I expected. Instead of papers and books strewn about from my incredibly busy comrade, his office was immaculate and well decorated. Noticing my surprised review of his surroundings, he explained.

"Trial is a meticulous puzzle. We already have the law on the books. So, master the facts and you win the case. It's as simple as that. And to master the facts, you must be organized. So I treat my office in an organized manner, and it helps me stay focused."

"It's a far cry from the disheveled book bag you used to lug around in law school," I replied, "but I can get used to it."

With a laugh, he asked how my research is going.

"Dre, when we last left off, you asked me to get hard evidence. Mission accomplished!"

He watched intently as I opened up the bag to remove the recording equipment Hatcher Taves had entrusted me with, placed the projector on his desk on the right corner of his desk, and plugged it in. I set up the screen a few feet away and mimicking Hatcher I said, "Hit the lights."

Dre turned off the lights, closed the blinds, and returned to his chair. He leaned forward to get a close view of the film's horrifying contents. Having watched it again, the images were no less disturbing to me. Dre seemed skeptical, but unfazed. In his line of work, he must be used to seeing the wretched acts of humanity, this was just another act in that long list. When the film ended, he turned on the lights and began with a litany of questions.

I explained that the film came from Hatcher, the son of the now deceased Maggie Taves. He was riveted to learn about his father's technological savvy in rigging a night scope used by soldiers of the Vietnam War onto a super 8-millimeter recording device producing a primitive, but obviously functional, night vision recorder. He studied the pictures I had taken of the murder scene, comparing them to Maggie's pictures with all their markings showing the same location.

"Notice the tree line to the right of the osprey platform aerie," I said. "The trees were much smaller there thirty seven years ago and the platform did not exist, but you can see the same background and the water from the bay in the distance."

He was intrigued about my stay at the scene of the murder well past dark, and how a full moon illuminates the area brightly, which was fully evidenced by the clarity of the film. Dre feverishly took notes and freely asked questions along the way.

We replayed the film for another viewing.

"Notice how the body was moving before the knife strikes down three times leaving it lifeless. And the film shows the parked vehicle, with the clearly identifiable New York license plate tag # *ESE9793*, while a view of the killer remained in the background during the entire time. There appears to be no editing, just raw footage."

"This is good," he said, "But it may not be enough. We would need evidence that can shed light on the identity of the perpetrator."

"I thought you'd say that," I said. "Admittedly, the truck may not exist anymore, but the license plate number is clear. If we can trace the plates, we may have a lead on the killer. Last night, I submitted an online application for an expedited Freedom of Information Request with the Department of Motor Vehicles. There is a 3-5 day wait on that, but hopefully it can yield some information on that vehicle. Is there any chance of me getting some help here, maybe a warrant or something?" I reluctantly asked.

Dre shook his head firmly to indicate no.

My friend's eternal skepticism tempered my excitement at the clear evidence before us, so I sheepishly asked what he thought.

"We could have problems with the film in court, if it ever got that far," he said. "The person who filmed it is dead. A good defense team will challenge its admissibility at trial because of their inability to cross-examine the witness. Without more evidence, I don't think I can get our office on board. But you are getting close, real close. Get me something on that vehicle and I think we can look into it. I already started funneling the idea to my boss," he said.

"Any interest?" I asked.

Dre just looked at me and rolled his eyes.

"Evidence, my man. Evidence."

"Well," I replied, "Like we used to say in law school, I'll hold the fort."

"Yes," he said. "Hold the fort. Get me a little more. If we finally have enough to go on, I'll promise you the cavalry."

For its protection, and my own sanity, Dre agreed to keep the film and equipment locked in his office.

Sitting in my car, my mind focused on the nature of my research. One true benefit so far is that no one really knows, or perhaps cares, that I am investigating a crime that took place nearly four decades ago. Other than the fear that was manufactured in my own mind, there has yet to be any real danger. After all, if they are still alive, the characters in this case are very old. This story is as buried to them as Maria's body was.

My private research is not without its serious drawbacks though, chiefly because my lack of law enforcement and prosecutorial authority makes it so much harder to attain evidence. One phone call from Dre would produce a complete history of the vehicle spotted in the film, which could potentially lead to the killer. Still, I trusted my colleague's intuition. Without a warrant, any evidence uncovered improperly would likely be suppressed at trial. This would undoubtedly send those involved in this crime, if there are any left, deeper into hiding. Even worse, it could spawn lawsuits against the department putting Dre's career in jeopardy.

Dre was right. For now, I had to continue on my own and keep gathering evidence, putting the pieces of this case together, and building the puzzle until the cavalry would come. There was no other choice. Although I may not have been working as an attorney in the way that I envisioned as a law school graduate, the skills that I've learned were being put to good use. Most of all, they were being used to help someone, even though that person had died violently 37 years ago. This, after all, was precisely my motivation for going to law school in the first place, and it felt good, damn good.

Now, as I left Dre's office excited at the prospect of getting assistance from the United States federal law enforcement, it was finally time to go to New York City to try to locate Lola Cruz. Even if she could found, I had no idea how to begin to tell her about the death of her poor mother.

# Contact

Since Lita's death, Lola continued to live in the same apartment she was raised in. The neighbors, many of whom were elderly and have known her all her life, appreciated Lola's pleasant demeanor, and she enjoyed their company. Lola often runs errands for her neighbors who in return reward her with long conversation full of stories of the Lower East Side. Lola loved history. She always paid sincere homage to the days gone past, and her neighbors had more than enough information to impart upon her.

Lola also spends a great deal of time with her neighbors at community meetings, railing against the proposed changes to the neighborhood by a group of wealthy donors who are backing a plan that would gentrify the neighborhood. With a tireless work ethic and deep conviction in her beliefs, Lola emerged as the leader against this campaign, which included having her go from door to door informing her neighbors of their rights. On this particular night, Lola returned home from a long day of campaigning. She hadn't eaten dinner yet, and work the next day was fast approaching. As she reached the long walkway up towards her building, she noticed a man leaning against the railed fence staring at her. The man didn't seem threatening. In fact, he seemed quite pleasant, but his inquisitive stare made her curious. Perhaps someone from the gentrification committee, she thought. Avoiding eye contact, Lola approached the entrance to the building and as she reached for her key to gain entry, the man stepped forward and said,

"Excuse me, are you Lola Cruz?"

Smiling, Lola said, "Yes, can I help you?"

Smiling back, the man said, "Hi, you don't know me. My name is Savoy Graves and I have some information about a woman named Maria Cruz who I believe was your mother. Can we talk?"

Stunned by the mere mention of her mother, Lola agreed to accompany Savoy to a small nearby tavern called the Bookstore. It was a trendy place that drew a combination of college students and middle-aged locals. Most of all, it was a public place, one secure enough to meet this stranger.

Without an easy way to raise the subject of her long deceased mother, Savoy removed a copy of the newspaper article from his pocket, and placed it on the table in front of her. Lola spent a few minutes reading the article. Her forehead wrinkled up with a combination of deep thought, and some pain, but she remained calm as she sipped her drink. Although it was no easy task to invade her life with this news, the look in her eyes confirmed to Savoy that he made the right decision to contact her.

Savoy explained who he was and how he had begun to embark on the journey of researching the death of Maria Cruz. He explained that Maria worked at the Rivington estate, and was reported to have had an affair with the youngest son of that family. He also told her that Maria was fired, and a year later had a child, a young girl, who must been no more than a few months old when Maria was killed. The only family on record, he explained, was a Juana Cruz and a woman named Nadia Lopez, who lived at the same address where he met her at earlier, and after asking a few of the neighbors, was told that Lola lived there and provided her description to him.

"Ms. Cruz," said Savoy, "I have every reason to believe that the little girl born in the North Fork in 1973 is you and that Maria Cruz was your mother."

Aghast at Savoy's words, Lola remained silent. Savoy already knew how hard this would be and instead of continuing to overwhelm her, he wrote down his cell phone number on a piece of paper.

"Call me if you want to talk more. If not, I would understand." Savoy finished his drink and left the bar.

Lola remained in the booth studying the article. Her mind was abuzz with thoughts of potentially learning the truth, some truth, about the death of her mother. For years, Lita told her only fragmented parts of her mother's life. However, other than the general story that her mother got sick and died when Lola was a baby, Lita never spoke about the circumstances of her death.

As Lola grew older, she needed more information. Lola always needed more information. This is an integral part of who she is. While knowing a little about her mother's life was helpful, it was never complete because she always felt that something was missing.

Lola is blessed to have one picture of her mother; a Polaroid taken at a beach somewhere in Long Island. In it, her mother is wearing a simple blue summer dress hugging the soon to be born Lola in her pregnant belly. Her joy was beaming. Lola has viewed this picture a million times in her life. Its image is forever ingrained in her mind. Like her mother, Lola has long wavy dark brown hair, full lips, and a radiant smile. She also has her mother's long statuesque legs and delicate hands. The similarities in their physical attributes give Lola great comfort. But without knowing more about her life, and death, the *void* always drowned out such comfort.

She recalled a line from a poem recited in one of her favorite movies *"The Crow."*

*"Mother is the name for God on the lips and hearts of all children."*

As beautiful as that verse is, it always haunted her, because for Lola, her God was alien to her.

Now, for the first time in her life, there may be some new information about her mother, her God. But who was this man, Savoy Graves? Lita had raised Lola with rock solid values, always to have a cautious eye towards men. She now wrestled with the notion of trusting him. Yet, why would a stranger go out of his way to research the case, get some evidence, and then locate her? She had little money, so it was unlikely to be a ploy to swindle her.

She looked at the phone number Savoy had left her, and struggled with the dilemma before her. She could dismiss her urges to learn more, tear up his number, and just continue on with her life. Or she could fully pursue the quest for more information. While she would prefer to choose the latter, the former is a much easier proposition, and seemingly far less painful.

Thoughts of her father invoked even greater mysteries, but she never thought too deeply about pursuing those. For years, Lita always told her that he was never part of the picture. He was a playboy who could not resist Maria's beauty to procreate with her, but too much of a coward to accept the responsibility of a child.

Here was a chance to learn more about her mother, and perhaps about her father as well, and a stranger by the name of Savoy Graves might be able to deliver it to her. This lit a fire in her mind and heart that began to rage without an end in sight.

Lola picked up her phone and dialed Savoy's number. He had been gone for no more than an hour.

"Mr. Graves" she said, "I accept your offer. I am prepared to hear everything you have to say, and I will offer my help in any way possible. But I have to say that it would be the cruelest thing on earth if are lying to me, and if you are, I would spend the rest of my life doing all I can to make you suffer. Is that understood?"

"Understood," he said. "And please, call me Savoy. I am driving back out to the North Fork now. I will call you tomorrow, and everyday thereafter, to fill you in on the latest details."

With both skepticism and anticipation, she thanked him before ending the call.

# Acumen

The next morning I showered and went to a local diner for breakfast. My appetite was voracious. As I awaited the hearty feast of bacon, sausages, pancakes and eggs, I checked my email, surprised to see one from the Department of Motor Vehicles. This could be a good start to the day.

I opened the attachment of the email to see the results of my FOIL request. The truck that is seen in the film is a 1970 FT-735 Off Road Camper with Vehicle Identification Number *F735-YO-R73021*. Surprisingly, the vehicle only had two owners on record. At the time of the murder in 1972, it was registered to a corporation named *Acumen Holdings LLC*. A quick corporate search showed that Acumen was a private security firm based in Riverhead, New York. Unfortunately, that corporation went defunct years ago. The only other owner of that vehicle is a company named Warshaw Welding, Salvage, and Metal Fabricators in Holtsville, New York, only 45 miles west of Greenport. Armed with this new information, my plan was to leave at mid-morning, when traffic is usually lighter, and pay a visit to Warshaw Welding in Holtsville.

The owner of Warshaw Welding is a short plump man named Murray Warshaw, who sat comfortably inside a small air-conditioned office at the front of a huge scrap yard. As he proudly explains, he has been running this business for some 60 years after a having falling out with his brother.

"Seems like a fine establishment you have here," I said.

I told Murray that I had an uncle who may have sold a truck here in the 70's and that I am trying to backtrack his footsteps for a family tree we are compiling. Completely disinterested, he asked if I have any information on the truck.

"Yes," I replied, as I showed him a copy of the Vehicle Identification Number.

Murray stood up and went to the corner of his office to check several file cabinets. He opened and closed each of them as if he were a surgeon searching for the right surgical device. He then removed a folder marked 1972.

"This place may look like a mess" he said with a smile, "But I assure you, we are well organized."

Murray looked through the folder and after a few moments, he said,

"Here. This is the deed of sale. We bought a truck matching that VIN number back on October 5, 1972." I double-checked the VIN number on the DMV report and it matched the one on the deed of sale. Murray continued to scan his finger down the page for more information, but my eyes had already found its target: the signature line of the seller. Luther Vale had signed it on behalf of Acumen Holdings. So not only was he the detective that seemingly sabotaged the entire investigation, but a truck, that can be seen on the film of the murder, can be traced to him. All roads are leading to this guy Luther Vale, I thought.

"Do you know what ever happened to this truck?" I asked.

Murray looked through the file and could find nothing to indicate that it was sold, either in whole or in parts.

"Looks like it could still be here," he said.

My eyes widened and I asked if I could look around for it.

"I would have to take you myself," he said. "It's pretty dangerous back there."

I followed Murray out into the lot. He was right; it is a dangerous place for someone just to wander around. It was littered with twisted and jagged steel. We started at one corner of the lot, which had a large pile of scrap with seemingly every piece of metal from every car known to man. The hope of finding parts of this truck was clearly not plausible. My only hope was to find it in one piece, but as we walked across Murray's mechanical graveyard, that looked less and less likely. Still, our search continued. We crossed to the other side of the lot where there was a metal shed spanning about 40 feet wide by 40 feet across.

"Some cars under there are still in one piece," said Murray.

We approached and saw many different types of vehicles and engine parts underneath the shed. Some vehicles were half covered by large black canvas tarps.

My frustration began to grow feeling as if I was chasing a ghost in a graveyard. Undeterred, we continued our search with poor Murray as my guide. Towards the rear of the shed, I noticed one vehicle fully covered by a large black tarp. I called Murray over to see if we could inspect the vehicle whose cover was weighted down by dust sediment that seemed to have been there a very long time. Murray lifted the cover off the vehicle creating a large plume of dust. I covered my mouth and nose for a moment, and as I focused my eyes on the vehicle, there, under the dirt and soot in the back of this graveyard, sat an orange and white pickup truck. We checked the make and model, and sure enough, the vehicle was a Ford FT-735 Off Road Camper. It was grimy and rusty, but the body was still in good condition.

As Murray removed the entire cover, I took pictures of the truck with my cell phone. Murray then opened the door, which creaked loudly confirming that it hadn't been opened in many years. I asked if he knows where I can find the Vehicle Identification Number.

"Sure," he said, "On these older trucks, they were fixed onto the inside of the driver's side door."

"Here it is," Murray said, as he spit onto the plate and wiped it off with a rag to reveal the information.

I leaned in for a closer look, knowing how critical this information is, and quickly scribbled down the numbers *F735-YO-R73021*;

the same number listed on the DMV report. Although it did not have the same license plates that it had while being filmed, I was staring at the very same truck that Luther Vale sold here 37 years ago; the same truck that is visible on the film the night Maria was murdered. This, I thought, is as hard as the evidence can get. I took one last picture of the VIN plate tag before Murray began to drag the cover back onto the truck.

Back at the trailer, Murray poured me a cup of coffee. It looked like oil sludge, but I drank it just the same.

"Say, Murray. Is that truck for sale?" I asked.

"I guess so," he said. "Hell, up until a few minutes ago, I didn't even know I still had it. Make me a good offer."

I nodded.

"Keep it under wraps until I return. I may just take it off your hands."

I sent Dre an email with the DMV report and all the pictures I had taken at Murray's lot. As I left, I called him to be sure that he received it. Dre was just coming out of trial and in a very good mood.

"Another bad day to be a bad guy" he said, "What's up dude?"

"Check your email my friend and call me back," I said.

Minutes later, he called back and told me that I will be hearing from him in a few days. I could barely contain my smile as I began the drive back to the North Fork.

# Crushed

Chet missed her terribly. It's been nearly a year since she was fired and his life hasn't been the same. He knew where she lived, often thinking about paying her a visit, but his courage always failed him. On this night, he followed her home after she left work. She looked as beautiful as ever. Just seeing her made his heart flutter. She pulled up near her apartment and exited the car. Even her gait had a goddess-like quality. He had a few drinks in hopes of settling his nerves as he questioned his next move. Should he approach? How will she react if he does? Or should he just drive away, and let it go? Why put himself through the pain, he thought.

Fighting against his better judgment, he decided to approach her just to say hello. He quickly exited his car, clumsily sneaking up behind to grab her waist just as she placed the key into her door. Maybe she would turn and embrace him, he mused naively. Instead, his touch startled Maria and she pushed away from the unknown presence, turned the key, and pushed into the apartment. She feared that it was Luther, who not too long ago attacked her in the parking lot near work forcing her to fight off his advances. Turning to face the intruder, she was relieved that it wasn't Luther, but she was shocked that it was her former lover. Even with her bewildered look, Chet had forgotten how much he missed those eyes until that moment as his feelings came rushing back.

Maria stood at the doorway stunned by his presence. Chet understood her surprise, but hoped that she would welcome him in. Then, someone entered behind her from another room. It was a much older woman he had never seen before. She was holding a young child in her hands. With a nervous voice, Maria asked the women to take the child back from the room they came from.

She turned back to Chet and said, "You should not be here."

He wanted to pour his heart out and profess his love for her, but he was speechless, distracted.

"Who was that child?" was all he could muster.

Seeking to soften the mood, Maria invited him in to sit down and talk. He refused and repeated his question. Sensing his impatience, Maria tried to respond, but she could only fumble her words. Chet again asked who the child was, although the question was now rhetorical as he seemed to sense the colossal turmoil that its answer was about to wreak.

Maria finally composed herself and began to speak.

"Chet," she said, "that little girl you saw is my daughter, our daughter."

Chet closed his eyes in disbelief, and said, "That cannot be."

"Chet," Maria replied, "you are the father. I learned of the pregnancy a few months after I was fired. As time went on, I realized that I wanted to have this baby, even if alone. I didn't tell you because I was afraid that you would think it was all a trick, or worse, that it would upset your family. So I had the baby on my own. Chet, the entire pregnancy and birth was easy. 'Baby-light' is what I called her. She is a joy, Chet. She has the best features of each of us."

With his hands in his eyes, Chet was flummoxed. Despite his riches and access to whatever he wanted, his life was guided by the one strict rule: do not bring shame to the family. He violated that rule with Maria and now, the greatest fear that could befall a Rivington has happened, and it was all his fault. Sensing his confusion and fear, Maria placed a hand on his shoulder to comfort him.

"It's all right Chet," she said. "I will raise her on my own. You can be part of her life if you want, but you don't have to be. I want you to know that."

"Chet, do you want to see her?"

"No," he replied.

The denial in his eyes shined like a beacon and with a broken voice, he said,

"How do you even know she's mine?"

Maria stared in disbelief at his question. She had long feared that he was destined to be just like his parents, but somehow she always held out the hope that he was different and could be a part of their lives someday. Now as he stood there in complete renunciation of their love, she knew then that it was not meant to be. Her eyes welled up with tears.

"Really, Chet. I thought what we had was special, but it turns out that you're heartless, just like your fucking family," she said. Maria's tears were now replaced with rage as she continued. "I pity you Chet. Your family looks down on us and yet you're the ones who have no idea what love really is. Get out of here and leave us alone." She then slammed the door in his face.

Chet stormed away from her apartment to his car where he began to sob while punching the steering wheel. He was torn between the anger and despair of not being with Maria, the love of his life, and the bone chilling fear that this woman, a former maid at his estate, had given birth to a daughter, his daughter, a Rivington. He knew what he had to do, but in doing so, he risked any hope of a future with Maria. But he saw no other option. He was still 20 years old and had a future in front of him. His parents counted on him. The crushing weight of responsibility lay square upon his chest, his shoulders, and his soul. All other options were ruled out. There was only one thing he could do. As he dried his eyes and drove out of the parking lot, Chet picked up the phone, dialed a number and when the person on the other end answered, Chet said, "Father, we need to talk."

# The Kill

The vulgar display of power defiled the beautifully moonlit night. At six foot four inches and well over 250 pounds, the hulking Luther Vale easily manhandled his diminutive counterpart. After levelling the first blow to the back of Maria's head, her limp body was easy to manipulate as he hogtied and threw her into the back of the truck. He drove quickly, but not so fast as to alert the attention of anyone. Never can be too careful, he thought, and he smiled at his self-absorbed shrewdness.

He drove for about 10 miles to the kill site; a place carefully chosen for its solitude. He pulled over to the side of the road. The bitch started to struggle. He liked that, as it empowered him even more. He grabbed her by the ankles and tossed her to ground. She almost had a good look at his face, but he had no worries, as he punched her in the face three times. They were good ones, he thought. Especially the first punch. It almost caved her nose to the back of her neck. She didn't expect that, and he thrived on it.

In full control, he proceeded to drag her body. Her helplessness aroused him. He could have fucked her right there or killed her just the same. Hell, he thought, she had her chance, but she had the nerve to reject him.

Maria tried to speak, but could only mumble.

"Shut up, bitch," he said. "This is your own fault. You should have thought about that before spreading your whore legs."

When he reached the site, he struck her again and laid her on the sheet of heavy plastic he had set up in preparation. With two good rolls and several long strands of duct tape, she was completely covered in the tarp. Then he gave her another kick for good measure. He could feel her ribs crack under his boot.

The car pulled up quickly, just as planned. He almost coughed from the dust that the tires kicked up, but he would never show such weakness. He pulled out his knife and drove it home three times, right to the heart. Bitch didn't stand a chance, he mused with delight. He looked up when he heard the voice.

"Good riddance!"

When his preparations began hours earlier, Luther knew he should have dug a deeper hole, deep enough to better conceal the body, but this part of the work annoyed him. Someone of his stature should not have to waste his energy digging holes, he thought. He figured that it was deep enough since it was in the middle of nowhere. Now, as he rolled Maria's lifeless body into the makeshift grave and finished placing the dirt on top of her, he felt satisfied with his work.

In a couple of days, he would return to fetch the baby. The plan was to bring her by boat to Connecticut to dispose of her there, and if the grandmother got in the way, she would suffer the same fate as her bitch daughter. It was a good night, a good night indeed, he thought, as he gathered his gear and headed home.

# The Cavalry

Murray Warshaw rested comfortably in his office. He spent much of the morning with two of his workers preparing some scrap in the yard to be hauled off to a local buyer. It was only 11:00, but Murray was already fixated on lunch; a bowl of some home-made chili. As his delicacy heated up in the microwave, he cleaned off his desk, which was littered with small auto parts, paper, empty coffee cups, and other random debris. He's been meaning to clean his desk for the longest time, but he always gets distracted. Now, with his workers out on the road, he had the place all to himself. He cleaned up his desk just enough to set the now heated bowl of chili in the center next to an ice-cold root beer. Murray Warshaw loved his root beer.

He picked up his overly large spoon and scooped up a glob of chili. It was heavy and meaty. Just the way he liked it. His mouth watered with anticipation, but as he raised his spoon, there was a knock on the door. Two well-dressed gentlemen walked in. They ruined his planned feast and Murray was not pleased.

"Yeah" he said, "can I help you?"

"Mr. Warshaw," said one of the two men, "My name is Special Agent Richard Ramos, and this here is Special Agent Andrew Haverstraw. We are with the Federal Bureau of Investigation."

Murray dropped his spoon splashing some chili sauce on his already dirtied shirt.

"Oh shit," he whispered. "There goes lunch."

"Mr. Warshaw," said Ramos, "We have a warrant to search a

vehicle that you currently have on your premises. Would you like to review that warrant?"

Relieved that they were not there to discuss his questionable tax filings, Warshaw, shook his head no.

"Sure be my guest. Which vehicle?"

"Please, let's step outside" Ramos replied.

As they exited his office, Murray was overwhelmed at the sight of dozens of agents pulling into the lot along with a mobile forensics truck. He was not used to such traffic here.

"Where do you want to search?" Murray asked.

"We have received a tip that there is an orange and white Ford FT-735 Off Road Camper located under a shed in the rear of the property," Ramos said.

"Shit," replied Murray. "A fellow was here just the other day asking about that truck. We found it covered in the back. Is he involved in a crime?"

Ramos stared hard at Murray.

"That is confidential information. But I do have a question for you. Did you accompany that man to see the truck?"

Murray nodded yes.

"And were you with him the entire time?" asked Ramos.

Murray again nodded yes, as Ramos continued.

"Since he came here, has anyone else come afterwards to inquire about that vehicle?"

"No" replied Murray. "That truck's been back there for years. I forgot we even had it."

"Fine" replied Ramos, "We are going to need you to provide a sworn statement."

"No problem," responded Murray who then asked, "Say, should I be worried about anything here?"

Ramos looked at him icily.

"If you've done nothing wrong, then you don't have to worry about a thing."

Murray wiped his forehead, which was sweating profusely, as

he accompanied Agent Haverstraw back to the trailer to provide a statement.

Since he started his research, Savoy Graves has been hoping for that moment when Dre could get on board and reopen this case. Unbeknownst to him, it has already started. The cavalry had finally arrived.

# Exodus

The Greenport train station was bustling, far exceeding its volume for a normal Wednesday. The fall season was fast approaching and many visitors were travelling from all over the New York area. Juana Cruz arrived early to purchase her ticket for the 11:45 am train bound for New York City. In her right hand, she carried one large bag and a large purse. With her left, she pushed her granddaughter Lola who rested comfortably in a baby stroller. All of their remaining belongings were left behind in their small apartment. Juana purchased her ticket and quickly made her way to a seat on the train. She placed her belongings on the seat next to her, holding Lola firmly on her lap. Her nervousness grew with each passenger that entered the train. She was cautious not to make eye contact with anyone.

Juana and her daughter Maria had formulated this contingency plan ever since Chet's visit where he learned of the birth of their daughter. If Juana had not heard from Maria for 24 consecutive hours, Juana was to take the baby, by train or by any other means necessary, to the home of her friend Nadia Lopez in New York City, and stay there until she heard from Maria again. Now it's been over 72 hours and she hasn't heard from Maria. Juana held out the faintest of hopes, but now she had far surpassed the limits of their plan and could wait no longer. The best-case scenario would be for Maria to contact her later. The worst case, well, that was a thought she did not want to consider at this moment.

At exactly 11:45, the doors closed and the train began to inch forward. Juana clutched Lola as the train began to pick up speed. Juana peered outside the window with a tear in her eye, wondering if this was the last time she and Lola will ever be in the North Fork. If it was, then her life would begin anew in a place far from there. She would have to accept the fact that she had lost a daughter, and Lola had lost a mother. Lola, now awake, began to stir and looked up at her loving Grandmother. Juana took out a bottle of formula and gave it to Lola, who drank it with a fervor before dozing off again.

"Pobrecita," she whispered. "Pobrecita."

# Torpedo

Chet Rivington is the sole owner of Shelter Asset Management; a private equity investment firm headquartered in New York City. He wasn't particularly hard to find, but in many ways the prospect of approaching Chet was more complex than meeting Lola. There are so many questions raised. Is Lola his daughter, and if so, is he aware of it, or even care? Or worse, was he involved in Maria's death? The possibility of the latter gave me great cause to be nervous. If a man of his wealth was involved in the murder, then he surely has the resources to keep it a secret. Still, if I remained at a safe distance, then I should be fine. Besides, I thought, I may never get through to him. With these questions swirling in my head, I placed a call to his New York office.

Of course, Chet was unavailable. I should have expected that a stranger calling out of the blue would not have direct access to a man of his stature. But when the representative on the phone asked what the nature of my call was, I was caught off guard. I lacked the corporate acumen to pretend that I had legitimate business dealings with him. Yet, if I offered nothing, it would certainly fall on deaf ears. There was only one thing I could say, the one thing that only Chet would know that could evoke a response from him, so I went for it.

"Please tell him that I am representing Maria Cruz from Orient, New York."

I left my number before hanging up.

The torpedo is in the water, I thought. I had little doubt that Chet would know the nature of my message, but I had no way of knowing whether or not he would contact me. Then, my phone rang. I answered somewhat cautiously to hear the woman of the same voice I just spoke with.

"Mr. Graves," she said politely.

"Yes," I replied.

"I forwarded your message to Mr. Rivington. He would like to meet you. Do you have a pen and paper?" she asked.

"Yes," I again replied.

"Please meet with Mr. Rivington this afternoon at the Sterling Yacht Marina in Greenport, New York. Look for his yacht docked at the marina. It is named '*Enchanted.*' Will you be able to meet him at 1:00 sharp?"

I looked at my watch, told her that I could, before thanking her, and ending the call.

A marina during the middle of a warm spring day will likely have many visitors in the area. This is the safest possible place for us to meet. And such a quick response suggests a real eagerness to meet with me. Maybe he wants to feel me out, I thought. A man of such wealth getting a call from a stranger about his dark past is something he could perceive as an extortion plot. Or, I thought optimistically, maybe he has been longing to hear from someone who knows about Maria. I looked again at my watch. In the next two hours, I will be meeting the potential lover of Maria Cruz and quite possibly Lola's father. This just got much more serious.

# Obscurity

Situated on the western end of the Long Island Sound is Hart Island. About one mile long, and a half mile wide, this island has a dark history in New York. Since the mid 1800's, the island was used as a Civil War prison camp, a psychiatric institution, a sanatorium for patients with tuberculosis, and a reform home for troubled boys. The island has also been used as a place to bury the dead who have no family or friends to claim their body. Hence, the island's nickname, Potters Field.

With no further evidence at their disposal, and the identity of the killer never to be found, lead detective Luther Vale pronounced on March 23, 1973 that the Maria Cruz murder case shall be closed. The scant evidence that was deduced from the crime was stored in the basement of the Southold Police Department where the records were subsequently sealed. For several months, public notices were advertised in various New York newspapers requesting family or friends to claim the body. It was arranged so that the only person who would be contacted regarding these notices was Luther Vale. Of course, the only person likely enough to answer these notices would be the Grandmother, and if she did, it would give him the chance to locate the child and finish her off.

It was a perfect backup plan, he mused. More importantly, it was required since he was unable to locate the child to finish his sinister deeds. Five days after he murdered Maria, Luther had broken into her apartment. Judging by the amount of personal belongings left behind, he knew that the Grandmother and child had left hastily. He briefly questioned how they could have been tipped off, but remained confident in his stealthiness. He had staked out Maria's apartment for weeks afterward. Once he saw new tenants occupy the space, it became clear to him that the Grandmother and child were long gone. Based on his observation, and with the perfect backup plan in place, Luther felt comfortable enough to declare that he had completed his assigned task of killing Maria's child as well.

Now, with the costs of preserving Maria's remains soaring, it was decided that the town could no longer house the body. On a rainy morning on June 13, 1973, the body of Maria Cruz was loaded onto a small boat and ferried to Potters Field, where it was unceremoniously buried in a mass grave on the northwestern corner of the island. Today, her remains lay with thousands of other unclaimed individuals, forever mired in obscurity.

# Enchanted

I arrived at the marina one hour early to study the layout of the area. As I had hoped, the area was bustling with people and many ships were docked. Twenty minutes later, I saw Chet's yacht sailing in. The *Enchanted* was amongst the largest of yachts at the port. The 120 feet custom-built vessel was painted white with wood trimming, and boasted several bedrooms, a lounge, an indoor dining space, and a special area on the aft deck for dining.

As I stood there admiring the fine vessel, I almost didn't notice the middle-aged man standing towards the rear of the vessel staring at me. Our eyes met, and there was no doubt that we instantly knew the identity of each other.

Once docked, a beautiful woman dressed in a tan business suit exited the vessel and approached me.

"Good afternoon Mr. Graves," said the woman with a British accent.

Detecting my quizzical look, she said, "You are Mr. Graves, aren't you sir?"

"Yes," I replied.

"Please follow me then," she said. "Mr. Rivington is quite eager to meet you."

I followed her onto the yacht unsure of what to expect.

Chet stood with his back to me looking out over the water.

As I approached, he said, "My family has sailed these waters for generations, Mr. Graves. We consider it our home."

I remained silent as Chet turned to face me.

"My assistant told me that you were asking about Maria Cruz," as he gestured for me to sit.

"Yes," I replied. "I came upon the story of her death and since I had some free time, I decided to research the case."

Interrupting, Chet said, "Free time? If you were still working at Powell & Mason, I suppose you wouldn't have as much free time to do such things."

I was unable to mask my surprise at him knowing more about me that I was comfortable with.

"Come now, Mr. Graves. I have not gotten to where I am in life without doing some research on my own. You are a long way from Sunnyside, aren't you?"

I looked on defiantly as he continued.

"Look, I don't have any information on Maria's death other than what's been reported. She used to work for my family years ago, before she was fired. A year later, she was found dead. A thorough investigation ensued and her murder was never solved. This is all I know."

"Tell me, Mr. Rivington," I said, "Were you ever questioned about her death?"

"Yes," he replied, "by the police."

"And who questioned you," I asked?

"Detective Luther Vale" he replied. "He questioned me, and as far as I know he questioned everyone in our home."

"But wasn't Detective Vale a friend of the family, and if so, wouldn't it have been a conflict of interest for him to investigate her death?" I asked.

"I don't know anything about that. I was 18 at the time," said Chet.

"There were also a rumored affair between you and Maria," I said. "Any truth to that rumor?"

Chet became visibly angry, stood, and said, "Mr. Graves, I am sorry, but I really have nothing more to offer you."

Just then, two very large men approached who were likely his bodyguards

Chet said, "I wish you luck on your future endeavors. You're familiar with the term, aren't you Mr. Graves? I believe it was written on your separation papers from Powell & Mason?"

Smug bastard, I thought. It became clear to me that his only purpose in meeting was to try to intimidate me. I stood to avoid the two men who reached to grab my arms.

"No need for an escort. I will see myself off."

As I turned to exit the vessel, I looked back at Chet.

"You know, she looks a little bit like you."

Chet stared at me with a puzzled look.

"Maria's daughter," I retorted.

I couldn't tell from his reaction whether he knew he had a daughter or not, but there was no doubt that my words cut him deep.

"She looks a bit like you. She kind of has your eyes. It's a pity that you have gotten to where you are in life by doing research on other people, yet are utterly unaware that you may have a daughter out there who is a lot closer than you think. Or maybe you do know and just don't care. That, sir, would be a shame!"

With that statement, I brushed past the two bodyguards and exited the yacht.

# Destiny

Lola arrived at Pennsylvania Station in New York City and boarded the 10:16 am Long Island Railroad train headed to Greenport to meet Savoy. Although he is still a stranger, she had no reason to distrust Savoy. It made no sense for him to exhaust his efforts chasing a story almost four decades old. And, as he had promised, he's called her on a daily basis to update her on the status of his research. During his call yesterday, he asked her to meet him in the North Fork so that he could personally share his latest findings with her.

Lola took a window seat toward the rear. She welcomed the three-hour train ride to collect her thoughts, which were ranging from anticipation to fear. She hadn't really thought what, if any, ramifications would come from Savoy's research, and it was unclear how far his investigation can go. Was her mother murdered, or did she really die of natural causes as she had always been told? After all, her mother's death happened so long ago. If she was indeed murdered, is it still possible for the killer's identity to be exposed, and if so, is he or she still alive? And what of her father's identity? If he is still alive, will she learn about him, or even get to meet him? These questions sputtered in her head like fireflies. Yet even if any of these questions are answerable, Lola questioned whether she was prepared to absorb the information they will bring.

The one certainty is that clinging to any potential information about her mother compounded her long suppressed feelings. Her entire life has been spent distracting herself from the *void*. Now, the truth behind that void is nearing and she doesn't know if she is brave enough to face what it may bring.

As the train made its way further east, Lola sensed her destiny fast approaching. Lita had often told stories about her mother, but without more, such stories were more like fairytales to her, both unknown and unreal. Since meeting Savoy, she had already felt a more tangible connection to her mother, more than she has ever known before. Clearly, the anticipation of finding the truth about her fate is the one thing she has longed for; the one thing that can bring about some measure of closure.

The train was now rolling through the bucolic countryside. From the distance, Lola could see the vineyards and vast farmlands. Such a beautiful place, she thought. She fantasized about taking a trip out here with her mother and Lita. For all the pain she has endured in her life, Lola was blessed to have been raised by Lita. She was a strong woman who preached solid values. Some of her fondest memories included trips with Lita to the market to purchase fresh poultry to make her famous soup. Lita always made extra soup to pass out to the neighbors, or even to strangers in need of a good home cooked meal.

Lola closed her eyes to her conflicting thoughts, slowly falling into a deep slumber. A short time later, the sound of the conductor's voice wakes her.

"The next and last stop on this train is Greenport."

Lola wiped her face, clutched her bag, and as the train came to a halt, she rose to meet her destiny, with, much to her surprise, more courage than she thought she'd have.

# Call to Order

The Board of Trustees for the town of Southold were conducting their quarterly meeting at Town Hall to a sparse group of residents interested in the Board's plans for the next calendar year. This was the last meeting before the onset of the busy summer season. Luther Vale sat fiddling with his cell phone at the end of the Trustees' table in front of the audience. He was completely disinterested, making no attempt to hide it. As the Board announced several different motions, Luther and the other Trustees robotically and unanimously stated "aye."

Luther has held this position for more than 30 years. It was one of the few lasting gifts bestowed upon him by his benefactors, the Rivingtons, for his many years of dedicated service. Now at 61 years of age, Luther is retired from the Southold Police Force with honors, and lives quite comfortably in Southold. He never married or had children, which was fine, because it allowed him to focus solely on his own aspirations and, in his mind, a position on the Board continues to affirm his power and prestige in the area.

The meeting continued with a session for residents to voice their opinions openly. One particular resident took the opportunity to rail against changes proposed by the Trustees to the municipal parking in the village. As the man carried on, Luther's disgust became readily apparent. He reviled troublesome residents who complained over petty things. They should shut up, he thought, and be happy with the services they get from living in this town.

"Fucking ingrate," he whispered under his breath.

Luther watched the clock at the rear of the hall with great intensity. For him, the end of this pathetic exercise in democracy could not come soon enough. As he peered out into the meager audience, he noticed someone he had never seen before. A white male in a suit, well dressed, was standing in the rear of the hall. The man focused his stare on Luther. With his bravado never to be outdone, Luther stared back. As several other residents spoke, Luther watched as the man moved from the rear of the room toward the outer aisle and slowly began to descend toward the front. He never took his eyes off Luther. Then Luther saw a second man also dressed in a fine suit, by the front row across from the Trustees' table standing near the exit. Luther was pleased to still have his keen law enforcement senses, but the presence of these two men made him uneasy.

As the gavel fell ending the meeting, Luther stood quickly to gather his belongings. He had no idea who these men were, but he wanted nothing to do with them. Luther stepped away from the table, hoping to blend with the crowd as they made their exit. As he spied the man to his right, he did not see the one to his left who quickly approached him and blocked his path.

"Luther Vale, my name is Special Agent Andrew Haverstraw. Do you have a minute?"

# A Cross to Give

Savoy met Lola at the Greenport train station where the two engaged in a long hug. They stopped for a bite to eat before going over to the Oyster Cove Inn. Savoy has reserved a small cottage for her to stay in, as the investigation was ongoing. Once settled in, they agreed to meet on the beach nearby. As they sat by the water, overlooking the landscape of Shelter Island, Savoy said,

"I have something to give to you Lola."

He removed the velvet bag from his pocket.

"John Conte was the first officer to investigate your mother's death. In his files he had this."

Savoy removed the chain from the bag and held it carefully to let the cross dangle for a moment before passing it to her.

"Your mother was wearing this the night she was murdered."

Lola's eyes immediately welled up in tears as she held the chain with delicate hands. For the first time in her life, she had a tangible object in which she can directly channel her mother's spirit.

Savoy took her hand.

"John Conte did all he could, but he was removed from the case and forced to retire. He told me to tell you that he is sorry that he couldn't catch the killer. From what I've seen, he did all he could. He is one of the good guys."

Savoy took the chain from her hands and gestured to put the cross on Lola. Lola gently lifted her long hair as he manipulated the chain around her neck. Lola closed her eyes and touched the cross for a moment before giving Savoy a deep hug of appreciation.

"Lola," said Savoy. "I have something else to tell you."

Before he could go into his encounter with Chet, Lola dried her eyes and interrupted him and said, "Yes, I want you to tell me everything."

She took his hand, and led him on a stroll along the beach.

# Swagger

Although he was not placed under arrest, Luther agreed to accompany the federal agents back to their offices in Melville, New York. Because he was a veteran of law enforcement, who retired with honors and a pioneer in his town, Luther feared nothing. They probably need him to testify in some trial or seek his counsel in a case, he thought.

The men entered the FBI headquarters and Luther remained relaxed, even cocky. It felt good, he thought, to be back in the law enforcement arena. They sat in a large room where he and Haverstraw engaged in a very collegial discussion. Luther regaled the young agent with his long history with a badge. Haverstraw was young and eager to listen. A newbie, thought Luther who immediately took a liking to the kid. And best of all, the kid is white. It's good to see his fellow comrades in law enforcement, he thought, even if he was a federal agent.

The friendly banter between Haverstraw and Luther continued for nearly half an hour. But now it was getting late, and Luther had at least an hour's drive back home. Before Luther could ask Haverstraw why they needed him, Special Agent Richard Ramos entered the room. Luther immediately sized up the agent. Everything about Ramos incensed Luther: the sharp suit, shined shoes, the razor edged sideburns, and the tight haircut. Even his perfectly manicured nails and the smell of his cologne offended Luther's senses. But the most heinous of offenses, the coup de grace of Agent Ramos in the eyes of Luther, was the fact that he was Hispanic. Over the years, Luther lost his ability to hide publicly his disdain for minority races. Those who wore a badge, especially federal law enforcement, piqued him the most.

Agent Haverstraw stood up to leave the room. Luther immediately detected their ruse. The classic good cop-bad cop routine, he thought, usually employed by law enforcement on perpetrators. In Luther's mind, they were attempting to soften him up with the friendly white guy, until the minority shows up. But Luther was not a perpetrator, or so he thought. In a show of true disrespect and defiance, Luther leaned back in his chair and placed his feet on the table. He turned towards Haverstraw as he was exiting the room, and with all the sarcasm in the world said,

"Have a good one, bro."

Haverstraw smiled and closed the door behind him.

Ramos sat at the table directly across from Luther. The two were not more than three feet apart. Ramos opened up his leather briefcase and methodically removed a file, a pen, and his reading glasses, which he placed on top of the file. Ramos also reached for a bottle of water from his suitcase and opened it for a long drink. Luther, remaining unfazed by the young agent's routine, was growing irritated, glancing at his cell phone until Ramos broke the silence.

"Mr. Vale," said Ramos. "I am federal agent Richard Ramos. My superior officers have sent me here to ask you a few questions."

Immediately cutting him off, Luther said, "So, I'm wasting my time with an inferior then."

Ignoring the jab, Ramos put on his reading glasses, opened the file, and remained silent for another moment to review it before he began his questioning.

"I'd like to ask you about your knowledge of the death of Maria Cruz in 1972," said Ramos. "We have obtained a copy of the complete file on this particular murder case from the Southold Police Force."

"A little late to the party, amigo," said Luther almost breaking into laughter. "That was a long time ago."

Luther again glanced at his cell phone and said, "Look, it's getting late."

Ramos ignored him and continued to study his paperwork.

Now incensed, Luther took his feet off the table, leaned in and barked, "Look junior, I've made my bones in law enforcement when your mama was wiping your ass. If you have something to say, then say it. Otherwise, it's time for me to get the fuck out of here."

Ramos continued to ignore him and Luther, now outraged, stood up to leave. Suddenly, there was a tap on the glass.

Instinctively, Luther sat back down as Ramos stood and said, "Please excuse me."

Five long minutes had passed before Ramos reentered the room.

Luther, whose patience was worn asked, "Are we about done here?"

Ramos, now smiling, said "Soon, very soon."

"Mr. Vale" said Ramos as he cleared his throat. "Approximately two weeks ago, our office received a tip on the whereabouts of a vehicle. An orange and white Ford FT-735 Off Road Camper."

Stone faced, Luther looked on.

"The vehicle is quite old, 38 years old to be exact with not many miles on it."

"What does this have to do with"…and before Luther could finish his question, Ramos continued.

"The truck has a seven foot rear flatbed, perfect for hauling many objects. A rare truck for its time. To ensure the vehicle's proper weight and to maintain maximum load space in the back, the vehicle is fitted with an extended wheel base, and because of that extended wheel base, the spare tire had to be stored in a side compartment that is only accessible on the outside of the flatbed. Again, acting on a tip as to the whereabouts of this vehicle, our office was able to obtain a warrant to retrieve it."

Luther rolled his eyes with indifference.

"Our crime lab is very good, Mr. Vale" said Ramos. "The best that the United States Government can provide. So, we had our crime lab tear into this vehicle with a fine toothed comb. In the right compartment towards the rear of the vehicle, they found, not so neatly tucked behind the spare tire, a burlap bag. The bag was extracted and its contents were carefully removed for inspection. Inside, the lab techs, they prefer to call themselves *"Bloodhounds"* because of their forensic prowess, inside they found crumpled pieces of duct tape. On the tape, they found black hairs still stuck to the pieces of tape. Isn't that something, Mr. Vale? After all this time, duct tape still has strong adhesive properties."

Luther clutched his cell phone as beads of sweat began to form on his forehead. He glanced over to the mirrored wall fully aware that their conversation was being monitored. He sat upright in attention, his swagger now gone.

Ramos continued.

"The hairs were sent to the lab, and we are expecting a report on them very shortly. In the bag, they also found, among small samples of soil a human tooth. The tooth is also being examined carefully, and will soon reveal its host. We are also testing the soil. We have technology that can pinpoint soil samples by geographical location. It's pretty amazing, really."

Growing agitated, Luther again tried to interrupt the agent, but Ramos would not be deterred.

"Lastly, inside the pile of dirt, the Bloodhounds found a partially torn patch from a work uniform. The patch was traced to a uniform that has always been worn by employees of the Oyster Cove Inn in Greenport, New York and its tears match the patch seen in the crime scene photos. It's got that distinctive mermaid in a seashell, you know. Mr. Vale, we have every reason to believe that all of this evidence will be directly traced to the murder of Maria Cruz."

The agent continued in a methodical fashion.

"The vehicle identification number of the truck was traced to only two owners. The first owner, and most relevant for our purposes, was a corporate entity named Acumen Holdings, a private security firm formed in Riverhead in 1972. A real smart name for a company, don't you think?" Ramos asked with a smile as Luther fidgeted in his chair.

"The vehicle was sold on October 5, 1972 to Warshaw Welding, Salvage & Metal Fabricators in Holtsville, New York."

Luther's eyes narrowed. He could not believe the amount of information they have amassed.

"The deed of sale" said Ramos "was located and the signature of the seller of the vehicle in 1972 was none other than a Mr. Luther Vale. Of course, we also conducted a thorough corporate search of Acumen Holdings. We have found that the owner, sole proprietor, and only employee of Acumen Holdings was, yes you guessed it, Mr. Luther Vale. The forensic evidence is due back very shortly Mr. Vale and it appears that we can trace this vehicle, and all its evidence of the murder, directly back to you.

"Also, we have a sworn statement from John Conte detailing your questionable activities during the murder investigation. I know that you are well aware of who he is. We also have a statement from Fred Thorne."

Sensing Luther's bewilderment at that name, Ramos said, "That was the farmer in Orient, who swears that you gave him the order to plow the field thereby eliminating forensic evidence from the crime scene."

Luther wiped his face, cleared his throat and defiantly said,

"You've got nothing on me. Conte is a hack who was thrown off the force twice and Thorne lied then and is lying now to save his ass. As for the vehicle, I'm not saying I did, but assuming I did own a truck like that, it hasn't been in my possession for nearly forty years. It won't hold up in court. Stop embarrassing yourself and stop wasting my time."

With that statement, Luther stood and headed for the door.

"Mr. Vale, I am not done yet," said Ramos.

Before Luther could reach for the door handle, Ramos said,

"*ESE9793.*"

Luther froze in his tracks.

"Yes, Mr. Vale," said Ramos. "Those were the plate numbers of a vehicle spotted near the field the same night that Maria Cruz was murdered."

Luther turned with widened eyes to listen closely as he sank back into his chair.

"I imagine you are wondering how we know that," said Ramos. "Well, we have in our possession an 8 millimeter film shot on the night of the murder. In it, a big guy, that fits your description, although much younger at the time, is seen dragging a woman across a field and stabbing her to death. The murder happened in the same location where Maria's body was found. Here's the kicker though. The person who shot the film had the gumption to get a close-up of the vehicle with the killer still in the background as he was burying the body. The vehicle is, yes, you guessed it, a Ford FT-735 Off Road Camper with license plate number *ESE9793.* The owner of the vehicle at that time was Acumen Holdings, and the only registrant of that vehicle was you. Oh, and the film, that was shot by Maggie Taves. You knew Maggie Taves quite well, didn't you Mr. Vale? It turns out that she wasn't so crazy after all," Ramos said with a wide grin. "Our experts have studied the film and have confirmed its authenticity."

"Now, Mr. Vale" Ramos said, "Is there anything you would like to tell me?"

Luther sat deflated and shocked. With reddened eyes, he cleared his throat, leaned forward in his chair and said,

"I want a lawyer."

With a wide smile, Ramos said,

"Sure, Mr. Vale. That is your right."

As he stood to exit the room, Ramos leaned in close to a visibly shaken Luther Vale.

"Mr. Vale, I have one question for you."

As Luther looked up at the agent, Ramos asked, "Who's inferior now, bitch?"

# Sting

Dre called and requested that he meet with Lola and me at my cottage at the Oyster Cove Inn. He pulled into the gravel parking lot in a black SUV accompanied by federal agents Ramos and Haverstraw. Their sharp suits and dark sunglasses did nothing to conceal the fact that they are FBI agents.

When they entered, I immediately informed them that I met Chet on his yacht a few days ago.

"He is a real pompous ass!" I said. "And then, to my surprise, he called the next day and said that he wants to meet me and Lola at his home on Shelter Island. I could tell that his tone had totally changed."

"We know," said Dre. "The calvary has finally arrived. We obtained a warrant and expanded our investigation to include the monitoring of all of Chet's telephone calls."

"Why didn't you tell me?" I asked.

"I didn't want to ruin the element of surprise," said Dre with a smile. "If you had known, you could have inadvertently tipped him off to our investigation. I promised you the cavalry; I didn't say we would be blowing loud horns. Not yet, at least."

Special Agent Ramos pulled his seat close to us.

"Here is the plan, Mr. Graves," Ramos said. "We will all ride out to together to the home. You will enter the home alone, while Lola waits outside at a secure location. For her own safety, under no circumstances will she be allowed to enter the house."

He looked hard at Lola and said, "Ms. Cruz, I know that this may be difficult for you, but we cannot place you in a situation that jeopardizes your safety. This is non-negotiable."

Lola nodded in agreement, as Ramos shifted his focus back to me.

"We will have agents covering the entire perimeter. We want you to wear a wire."

Agent Haverstraw prepared the apparatus to be fitted under my shirt, while Ramos continued with his instructions.

"We need you to try and get Chet to speak about his association with Luther Vale."

"I knew that son of a bitch Vale was involved. What if Chet doesn't let me in? He specifically asked for Lola too?" I asked.

"As long as he believes that she is coming, or thinks she may be nearby, then he should let you in and hopefully let his guard down," said Ramos. "If not, then we'll take him anyway. We already have a warrant and we can let our legal eagles handle it," as he raised his hand and patted Dre's shoulder.

Dre looked at me hard and said, "Are you sure you're up to this?"

"Too late to turn back now," I replied as I looked at Lola. "Besides, I sensed a shift in Chet's tone from arrogance to...I don't know, maybe some sort of remorse or acceptance."

"Regardless of what you believe his state of mind to be, Mr. Rivington is a very volatile individual. So our agents will be right there if you need us," Ramos said. "If you sense any danger, they will storm the house within seconds after you say the code words."

"What are the code words?" I asked.

Dre looked at me in the eye and said, "Remember the code words we texted to let each other know if we passed the bar exam?"

"Al Bundy?" I asked in astonishment. "Really?"

The lead character of the popular sitcom show "*Married With Children*" was a favorite television show of ours, and while it was a humorous code between friends, it did not seem appropriate now with my life potentially on the line. Dre and Ramos studied my worried look until they broke into laughter.

"Just trying to bring some levity to the situation," said Dre.

Then Ramos added, "If you sense any danger, say these words: '*Do you think you will ever leave Shelter Island?*' Once those words are spoken by you, our agents will come crashing into the home, and when they do, get down and stay down until we tell you otherwise. Do you understand these instructions Mr. Graves?"

"Yes," I replied.

I stood, looked at Dre, shook my head, and laughingly said, "Al Bundy."

I sat in the back of the SUV between Lola and Dre as we took the short ride and boarded the ferry to Shelter Island. I had not realized it at first, but during the entire ride, Lola and I were holding hands tightly. It was clear that we were channeling our inner fears over what was about to happen in the next few minutes. I was facing a potentially life threatening encounter, and she was facing the prospect of meeting the father she never knew. I assured her that everything will work out and that we were in good hands with Dre and his team of agents.

As the ferry docked, we took the short ride over the Rivington estate. Before exiting the car, I gave Lola a hug, and fidgeted with my shirt to ensure that the wire was firmly affixed underneath. I approached the house slowly, and when I reached the doorway, a loud buzzer sounded, allowing me to push the door open. Someone in the house was clearly watching my approach and although Lola wasn't with me, I was still allowed entry. This, I hoped, was a good sign. The woman with the British accent who escorted me onto the yacht appeared and led me down a long hallway to a large door. She quickly knocked, opened the door, and gestured for me to enter before closing the door behind me.

Chet sat alone near a large oak desk positioned towards the rear of the large room. He had a drink in his hand and a serious look on his face. I quickly scanned the room. To his right was a marble fireplace, and to his left were two oversized windows. The room was dark and quiet. Chet gestured for me to come closer and sit down. As I approached, I quickly spotted a handgun positioned on the desk near his right hand.

Sensing my fear, he said, "Relax Mr. Graves. If I wanted to kill you, I would have done so already. Please, have a seat."

Chet offered me a glass of scotch, which he poured with shaky hands. I sat and we gave each other a long look. His bloodshot eyes then focused on an empty glass beside a near empty bottle of scotch.

"So," he said, "Where is she?"

Judging by the gun and a near empty bottle of scotch on his desk, I knew I had to tread lightly.

"She is not quite ready to see you yet, Chet," I said. "She needs some more time."

"It doesn't matter anyway," he snapped as he took another swig from his glass. "They would never let me be with Maria."

I watched him intently not wanting to interrupt his lucid moment.

"We were always one of the richest of families on Shelter Island, atop the elite social circle in the entire North Fork. All our moves were scripted...they had to be. But from the first minute I saw Maria, I was smitten. I never paid attention or even noticed any of the employees in the home before, but there was something special about Maria. She was demure, yet confident. She was... exotic. I have never seen anyone like her before, even among the richest of women in our society."

Chet poured some more scotch into his glass. He then opened his top drawer and pulled out a small glass mirror with cocaine on it. He used a razor blade to cut the cocaine into two long lines and snorted each of them with a small tube.

He wiped his nose, had another drink, and continued.

"Maria was beautiful. Her hair was always in a bun, but when it was let down, it was long and wavy. Her eyes were deep and commanded full attention. Her body was lavish and she always moved with an exotic grace, yet subtle, always subtle. Here was this fabulous woman, probably from a dirt poor family, yet with a royal mystique."

With the bottle of scotch now empty, Chet stood and went to the bar to retrieve another bottle. I gazed briefly at the gun, judging its distance. Too far, I thought, as Chet returned with the new bottle and plopped into his chair.

"Maria was always sweet," he said. "And proper. The first time she caught me looking at her was by the pool. I watched her cleaning off the patio table. She caught me looking and when our eyes met, she blushed, and quickly turned away. Over time, glances led to stares, and it wasn't long before I created opportunities just for us to be alone. What do you expect from a kid who was smitten? I've had plenty of sex before, but I never knew desire before Maria. To me, she was an exotic queen."

I sat erect in my seat to ensure that his words would be clearly recorded.

"One day I snuck up behind Maria in the library as she was dusting off some books. I placed my hands on her hips and she turned to slap me. Stunned, I quickly apologized, and she politely accepted. She apologized, too, but told me not to touch her like that. We then struck up some conversation. She spoke of her upbringing and asked about my interests. I spoke of foolish things that rich boys do while growing up; things like tennis, swimming and yachting. All that pretentious bullshit! Yet when we spoke, the social disparity between us dissolved. She took great interest in my experiences, as I did to hers. And then she smiled. I had never seen her smile before, but when she did, the room lit up. It was captivating and warm. I was hooked."

Chet took another drink of scotch and snorted some more cocaine.

"Days and months passed as we grew closer. Maria and I shared private glances and enjoyed our secretive talks. The sexual tension grew between us, but we didn't act upon our feelings. She always had this way about her that commanded my respect."

He looked up to the ceiling.

"God, if my parents heard me say that, it….."

He never finished that thought, but instead said, "There was no way in hell that my parents would have ever approved of Maria. She was part of our staff and fraternizing with the staff was strictly forbidden."

Chet took another swig of scotch and yet another snort of cocaine. I was astonished how his repeated use of this concoction didn't seem to affect his senses. He then rose to peer out the window completely unaware of the federal agents hidden nearby.

"Maria and I could be apart no longer," he said. "We slipped away whenever we could to make love. I still remember that one incredible night. We met by the pool, slipped off to the beach, and made love. Mr. Graves, most boys that age meet a girl and fucks her. With Maria, it was love. I have never been able to recapture such passion."

Chet returned to the desk, as I remained silent.

"I snuck off ahead of her and entered the house," he said. "It turns out that my bitch of a sister saw Maria and me out on the beach and told my parents. That was it. All hell broke loose. The next day Maria was fired. Gone, just like that," as he snapped his fingers.

"I was a fool to think that we could have been together. It was nothing more than a cosmic bet," he said as he reached into the drawer, took out a bag of cocaine, poured some of it onto the mirror, and snorted a larger amount than before.

"I was miserable for months," he continued. "I would hook up with some of the local girls, but none of them would come close to making me happy. My grades in school suffered. Life really sucked."

"I found out where Maria lived and for months I wanted to visit her. But how could I?" Then one day, I got up enough courage and went to see her. Like a fool, I thought it would be the same, but it wasn't. I could see it in her eyes as she stood at the door of her

160

apartment. Then something else caught my eye. A woman came from the other room holding a baby. I asked over and over again, but deep down I knew who it was and where she came from. She had my eyes."

Chet paused to take a long drink.

"I knew I was in a world of shit. I called my father to tell him the news. I had feelings for Maria, strong feelings, but a kid my age, under that kind of pressure, had no chance."

Breaking my long silence, I asked if he knows who killed Maria. He took a long swig from his drink.

"I did not kill her, Mr. Graves. It was that piece of shit Luther Vale. He did it. That snake would sell his mother's soul for a dollar and a slight amount of prestige."

"Did he act alone?" I asked.

"Mr. Graves," he replied, "You seem like a smart man. Listen to what I've already told you and you will figure it out."

I wanted to press for more, but I can sense his reluctance.

He then said,

"Luther Vale killed Maria. But in failing to protect her, I may as well have done it myself. Instead of warning her, I got drunk and fucked Molly Swanson that night. She wasn't even a good lay," he said with a warped laugh.

"What about the baby?" I asked.

"He was supposed to kill her, too. That's all I knew," Chet said before continuing. "Mr. Graves, my whole life has been spent living with this secret. I don't want it anymore. That is why I am telling you all of this. My life ended the night my love with Maria ended, and it sure as shit is over now that I know that my daughter had survived only to grow up without ever knowing her parents. I imagine that she will hate me for what I did. It doesn't matter. She can't hate me more than I hate myself, and I can't change what happened. Besides, I don't deserve her love. I wasn't man enough to save her mother or protect her. When you leave this office, I'm going pick up this gun and blow my fucking brains out."

Chet reached into a desk drawer and removed a large manila envelope.

"Here, take this," he said. "Give this to her for me. There are documents inside that tell the whole story."

He paused for a moment, looked at me, and asked, "Mr. Graves, what is her name?"

"Lola," I replied without hesitation. "Her name is Lola Cruz."

I studied the gun in Chet's hands and the look in his eyes. He was already gone, and it wasn't just the grams of cocaine he has snorted, or the bottles of scotch he drank. It was his guilt and despair. Yet, committing suicide would allow him to escape the justice he so badly deserves. I knew I had to distract him long enough for me to use the code words to send in the cavalry. The only way to do that was to play on his arrogance.

With careful thought, I said, "Chet, Lola is a wonderful woman; the kind that sees a whole lot of good in just about everything. The way I see it, there is nothing good that comes from her even acknowledging your existence. But, we'll leave that decision up to her. As for me, your words are just a pathetic attempt to justify the pain you've caused. As poor Maria's life was brutally snuffed out and her daughter, your daughter, was cast into a world of turmoil, you were fucking rich girls, attending the best schools, having posh parties and living carefree. Remember this Chet, she may not always pay on time, but justice always pays her bills. And you, sir, owe a mighty big fucking bill!"

Still pawing the gun, Chet stared at me. It was a risk to anger him in this state, but I had no choice.

"You know Mr. Graves," he said, "I've underestimated you. I don't know if you're crazy, stupid or have no life, but it took a lot of guts to do what you've done here. Now take this," as he picked up the envelope from the desk, "and get out, before I shoot you first."

As I reached for the envelope, I looked around the office pretending to take in all its splendor.

"Tell me, Chet, your family has been here for a long time. *Do you think you will ever leave Shelter Island?*"

Within seconds, two agents crashed through the windows, as I dove down below the desk with my arms folded over my head. In an instant, three other agents brandishing guns crashed through the door and into the office with one screaming,

"Drop it. Don't fucking move."

With his reflexes impaired by the mixture of drugs, alcohol and fear, Chet froze as two of the agents had subdued him forcefully. No shots were fired and Chet Rivington, who seconds earlier attempted to commit suicide because of his part in the heinous crime so long ago, was taken into custody for the murder of Maria Cruz.

# A Glimpse

Chet was bound in handcuffs and accompanied by two federal agents who led him out of the home. As he exited, he squinted his eyes at the bright sun that began to set over Shelter Island. The warm sun gave him a sense of freedom, the type he hadn't felt since spending time with Maria. The prospect of incarceration had little effect on a man who moments ago was prepared to take his own life, but the real source of his "freedom" was finally confessing to everything.

Lola sat nervously in the back of the police car, studying the grounds of the home where her mother and father had likely met. She contemplated what it would have been like had she entered the house to meet her biological father. It wouldn't have mattered, she concluded. He will forever remain an insurmountable mystery, whether she was one million miles away or right outside his door.

Lola turned her head when she heard the commotion, and out of pure impulse that she could not explain, she exited the vehicle and looked toward Chet who immediately spotted her. For the first time in her life, she stared directly into the eyes of her father. There was one other time of course, but she was far too young to have remembered, and he was far too much of a coward to have acknowledged it. Lola could only stare at him with a mixture of anger and compassion. Chet could only offer a brief and awkward smile in return as he thought that Savoy was right. She does have his eyes. As he sat in the car, he looked back at her mouthing the words "I'm sorry" before being driven away.

Savoy approached Lola and the two hugged each other for a few long moments. The strength of her grip let Savoy feel the depth of her emotions. They broke their embrace, and Savoy studied the poor woman's face before suggesting that they sit on a nearby bench overlooking the Gardiner's Bay.

"I have something to show you," he said as he handed her the manila envelope.

Out of safety concerns and for evidentiary purposes, the manila envelope had to be inspected by federal agents before Lola could review it. Once cleared and given to her, she held it loosely in her trembling hands. So many possible answers lied within, and she was not sure if she was ready to face them. A federal agent stood nearby, close enough to ensure the protection of what will likely be key evidence, but not too close to infringe upon her privacy. Savoy stood, offering to give Lola some privacy, but she grabbed his hand and insisted that he stay.

"If it weren't for you," she said, "We wouldn't be here now."

Savoy offered a brief smile as he sat down beside her.

As she opened the manila folder, the first document she read was a copy of Chet's recently amended will, which named his biological daughter to receive his share of all of the family's wealth. Attached to the will was a notarized letter signed by Chet offering his admission to his part in the murder of Maria Cruz Although he did not have a hand in the murder itself, or the planning of it, he was aware of it, and did nothing to protect or warn Maria. This, he felt, made him complicit in the murder itself. In the letter, Chet also requested to have DNA extracted from his body to confirm that he is in fact Lola's father. Of course, that was written with the expectation that he would have committed suicide. Now, fully alive and in custody, he would have no choice but to consent to a paternity test.

The second document was a Trust fund established in the name of his biological daughter in the amount of $17.3 million, to be distributed in lump sum upon confirmation that he is in fact her father. It appeared to be one last jab at denial by a Rivington. Attached with the Trust Fund was a short note to Lola from Chet which read,

*"All my life, I have never found true happiness. Except once, and that came from the time I spent with your mother. You may not believe it, but your mother and I loved each other and you are the only good thing ever to come from it. You will never understand what it was like to be in my shoes. That is not an excuse. It is just a fact. I cannot begin to tell you how sorry I am. My life has been filled with nothing but guilt, and once I learned that you were alive, I could not bear to face it any longer. Please take this money, as it is all I have to give to you. Use it as best as you can to replace everything that was taken from you. Love, Dad."*

Lola peered out over the bay in deep unfathomable thought.

For the next hour, Lola and Savoy sat on the bench as federal agents poured into the house to collect the weapon, the drugs, and any other evidence to indicate illegal activity. Much of the time was spent in deep thought, and even deeper conversation. Afterwards, they were driven back to the Oyster Cove Inn. Dre had requested that they remain in Greenport as he expected some more information on the case very soon.

This journey had no doubt created a deep affection between Lola and Savoy, one borne of the heart, but not yet acted upon or spoken of, between the two. They were simply too invested mentally and physically with the case to act upon such mutual feelings. Although they've been staying in separate cottages since Lola's arrival, the two now lay in his bed holding each other until they both fell asleep.

The next two days Lola and Savoy enjoyed the scenery of the North Fork and each other's company. Laura Wendt spent hours telling Lola stories of her mother, and of how they met when Lola was just a few months old.

"You had the cutest cheeks," Laura fondly recalled.

Lola removed the picture of her mother from her pocket and showed it to Laura.

"This is the only picture I have of my mother," Lola said.

With a wide smile, Laura said,

"I took that picture. She was so happy. She did not have enough time to enjoy you Lola, but there is no doubt that she loved you very much."

Now both in tears, the two women gave each other a long embrace.

"Thank you Laura," said Lola. "Thank you for being an important part of her life, and my life too."

The next morning, Lola arose and put some coffee on. She went over to wake up Savoy and the two walked down to the beach. It was a beautiful sunny day with a slight breeze. Their serenity was interrupted when Savoy's phone rang. It was Dre.

"Luther Vale provided a full statement, and it's pretty damning. We now have a name and an address," he said. "I have agents heading out there now. Meet us there within the hour."

Savoy looked at Lola and said, "We have to go. I'll explain on the way."

# Retribution

Sarah Forsythe Rivington has lived a long and prosperous life. Her husband Winston provided for her and the couple raised two fine children. The family enjoyed a life of excess. As they aged, her children ventured out on their own, leaving only her and Winston to enjoy the twilight of their lives until Winston died several years ago of a massive heart attack. He had his shortcomings, but he was the only love she had ever known, and she missed him dearly.

Now at 74 years old, Sarah Rivington spends her days in the Osprey Heights Nursing Home in East Marion, New York. Her declining health, which requires constant medical attention, forced her children to place her here. Of course, this is not just an ordinary nursing home. Only the wealthiest can afford this place. The immaculate facility, one built out of stone and glass, offers splendid views of the majestic Long Island Sound and a farm that harvests natural lavender. Each resident enjoys oversized individual suites with only the best of amenities and their own personal attendants.

Today, like every day, Sarah was resting comfortably in her room, watching her favorite soap operas and studying the menu for the day's meals. She had just been bathed by her trusted resident Gloria, and was in a pleasant mood. Sarah was certainly not expecting any company, and was surprised to see me enter her room.

"Good afternoon Mrs. Rivington, my name is Savoy Graves."

And before I could utter another word Lola, who had entered behind me, placed her arm around my waist, and said,

"And I am Mrs. Graves."

I looked at Lola quizzically, but played on as I continued.

"My wife and I are here touring the area and, as we so often do, we are paying a visit to places like this to say hello and..."

Lola cut me off.

"What my darling husband is trying to say is that we visit nursing homes and hospitals hoping to spend some time with people who could use a friend."

Lola looked at me and with a wink.

"Honey, please go to the car and get some of those fine pastries we packed. Mrs. Rivington and I will get to know each other a bit more."

Completely dumbfounded, I smiled at both women, and exited to the car.

"How are they treating you here, Mrs. Rivington?" said Lola.

"It's adequate I suppose," said Sarah. "Nothing could ever compare to being home."

"Is there anything we can do to help, Mrs. Rivington?" asked Lola.

"Sarah," she said. "Please call me Sarah. Well, I would like to get out of this stuffy room. Can you please help me?" as she reached for her cane.

"Sure," said Lola. "Let's go for a stroll."

Arm in arm, the two women exited the room.

"So, Sarah," asked Lola, "Do they offer many activities here for the residents?" "How about music, do they play music?"

"Yes," replied Sarah. "We have some exercise activities and play board games. But they don't play enough of Bach and Chopin; music that I love."

"Really?" said Lola, "That's a shame. I have read somewhere that classical music soothes the mind and helps with healing. Expecting mothers sometimes place headphones on their bellies for their babies to hear the music while in utero, although I imagine it would be tough to walk around with headphones on your belly?"

Sarah managed a chuckle at that thought, as they continued on their slow walk.

"Sarah, do you have any family that visits you here?"

"Sometimes," Sarah said. "But ever since my husband died and my children stuck me in this God forsaken place, I hardly see them. There are some nice people here, but nothing replaces family. Family is everything. You know what I mean?"

"I sure do," replied Lola.

Lola and Sarah proceeded into a courtyard outside the building where the two chatted away on a bench overlooking the Long Island Sound in the warm spring day. With pastries and a tray of tea in hand, Savoy returned to join them. He was uneasy with the situation and unsure how to proceed. Lola gave him a wink and a smile, which eased his nerves, and then, sensing their need to be left alone, he excused himself to use the restroom.

"That is a fine man you have there," said Sarah. "He sure is," mused Lola as they both watched Savoy reenter the building.

"Tell me about your family," said Lola.

"Well, my husband Winston died several years ago. He was the love of my life. Handsome and rich. He was a bit of a ladies' man, a fact I struggled with for a long time, but he gave me a good life, so I can't complain."

Sarah took a nibble of one the pastries before continuing.

"We worked hard to preserve what we had. With our wealth and family name, there were many seeking to latch on. This was especially the case with our son Chet. We were always watchful of the ladies that tried to enter his life. We worked hard to keep his focus on his studies instead of chasing pretty girls all the time. Today he's a well-to-do business man in the city; a product of the best education money can buy."

With her frail hands, Sarah raised the cup to her lips and sipped some tea before continuing.

"Our daughter, Rosemary, well, she has had her fair share of struggles in life. We encouraged her to seek more suitors, but none of them was ever able to live up to our values. Those that did were doomed once they got to learn her true personality. She is a hard woman, our Rosemary, with a cold heart and sharp tongue. I worry about her. We always did want grandchildren, but our children had high values to live up to, and that made finding suitable partners for them very difficult indeed. Still, our wealth has allowed us to be happy, even without the trappings of an extended family and future heirs."

"How about you my dear?" asked Sarah. "Do you have any children?"

"No, not yet," replied Lola. "I am getting older, but I do want children. I am lucky to have found the right man, though," as she looked toward the glass door where Savoy had exited.

"You are a fine young woman," said Sarah. "I am sure it will work out for you."

"Do you think so?" asked Lola.

"You are a wonderful well-mannered woman. You must have been raised by fine parents."

With a smile, Lola said, "It's my mother. She's an angel."

Lola then looked at her watch before continuing,

"Oh my, we have to move on. We have a busy day with other people to visit."

Sarah smiled.

"I cannot thank you enough my dear. This was nice."

Lola stood and helped Sarah up to her feet, and the two continued to chat during the long slow stroll back to her room.

As they reached the room, Lola helped a now fatigued Sarah back into her bed.

"Such a sweet thing, you are," said Sarah. "What did you say your name was again?"

Smiling, Lola leaned in to give Sarah a gentle kiss on her forehead.

"Lola. My name is Lola Cruz. And it was nice to meet you too, Grandma."

Sarah's eyes widened in disbelief and her veins strained in her neck.

"How can this be?" asked Sarah, who all this time thought that Lola was dead.

But one deep look into her eyes, and she knew for certain that it was true.

Now defiant, Sarah said, "Let me make you understand something girl. In our world, a relationship between my son and your mother would never have worked. He would have been an outcast and I would never have let that happen."

"It's strange," said Lola, "You said earlier that family is everything. You are right, except you have a warped definition of family. It is not about protecting the wealth and legacy of the family name. It is about allowing your family to grow through love and compassion and acceptance; all things you truly lack. And look at you now. Left to rot here without a husband, your children, nor a home. So much for your so-called world."

Sarah turned away, hoping to drown out the blunt truth of Lola's words, but she could not.

"I was a helpless little baby when you had my mother killed just to spare your precious family name. The love that my mother gave to me in that short time is far greater than any love you can claim to have had with your family for generations. Shame on you and shame on your family! Soon, you will have to answer to a higher authority, one more powerful than anything in this world. Good riddance, Sarah."

Now in tears and with a heavy heart, Sarah opened her lips to speak, but before she could utter a word, Lola exited the room. As she did, two federal agents entered the room to inform Sarah Rivington that she was under arrest for the murder of Maria Cruz in 1972.

Lola left the building riding the wings of justice.

Savoy rushed up to her.

"How'd it go?"

"Wonderful, just wonderful," said Lola, "I killed her with kindness."

The two entered the car without a need for words, because they both knew that there was one last stop to make.

# Wrath

It was a dark day in the Rivington household as Chet had just confessed to his parents about his affair with Maria and that she has conceived a daughter that was likely his. He now stood silently in the library with his parents and his sister awaiting their verdict. His cheeks still stung from the slaps of his outraged mother.

"A maid" she said. "Really? And now a bastard child! How can you have brought such shame to this family?"

A much more reserved, but no less irate, Winston looked at his son with extreme disappointment. Chet was smart enough to say nothing. He would have to accept any punishment they would levy upon him. Rosemary stood nearby, pleased by the results of her guardian duty. After all, she was the one who informed their parents of Chet's filthy affair almost a year ago. Winston instructed the children to leave the room so that he may consult with his wife.

Attempting to appease the outraged Sarah, Winston mixed his wife a cocktail, handing it to her.

"Sarah, our son is a just a boy who made a mistake. We'll pay the girl off to keep it quiet."

His words did nothing to quell her fury. Sarah placed the drink down on the nearby coffee table, looking at him coldly.

"Winston, I have never known another man other than you. I have given my blood, sweat, and tears for this family. And all you have done to repay my devotion is fuck your filthy whores. For too long you have taken me for someone so ignorant that I should turn a blind eye to your infidelity."

"Oh, please woman," he retorted. "Must we go over this again? Have I not paid for my transgressions? This is not about me, this is about our son."

Undeterred, Sarah continued.

"Has your heart grown so cold that my suffering no longer commands your respect?" she screamed. "You have pierced my heart too often, and that is a trait you have now bestowed upon our children. I will have no more of it."

Stirring the ice in his drink, Winston looked on nervously. The woman would have her say, he thought, and nothing will stop it.

"Now my husband," she said, "you will now answer to me. It was I who have kept this house, and the Rivington name, clean. It was I who was made to suffer with a broken heart from a cheating husband, forced to put on the airs of a warm home. By God, my efforts will not be in vain. I will not allow our son to follow in the crooked footsteps of his corrupt father. My wrath will no longer be stifled. Do you have any idea what would happen if that bitch and her bastard child exposed this secret?"

"I have committed my fair share of sin, it's true," he said, "But this is different. We will work this out."

His words had no effect on his seething wife.

"I want that bitch dead," said Sarah with a demonic look in her eyes.

"Come now," said Winston. "Isn't that a bit drastic? The right sum of money will..."

Interrupting him, she repeated her demand more loudly.

"You're talking about murder! There are other ways to handle this."

Without hesitation, Sarah threw her drink across the room against the wall, shattering the glass. She looked at him sternly

"I want her dead. I will not have that filthy whore tarnish the Rivington name and render my efforts meaningless. I will have my vengeance, by God, or for as long as I breathe air on this earth, I will make your life a living hell. You will rue the day you were ever born. With my tongue, I will burn the precious Rivington name, and watch your legacy burn to ashes. I will do this before that whore exposes us. This I swear to you."

Winston stood to console his now sobbing wife. He knew what had to be done. He summoned Luther to join them in the library, and in that dark cold room, they hatched their diabolical plan.

"There is one condition," said Sarah. "I must be there when you kill her. Is this understood?"

Luther nodded in agreement, as he started for the door.

"One more thing Luther," added Sarah. "When it is done, you are to dispose of the child too. Is this understood?"

Luther paused to look at Winston, who could only hang his head in deference.

"Consider it done," said Luther before exiting the room.

As he did, Luther was surprised to see Chet standing near the slightly ajar door, allowing him to hear his parents conspire with Luther Vale to murder Maria Cruz and their child.

# God

The sun was beginning to set over the North Fork as Lola and Savoy reached their final destination; the site where Maria's body was found in Orient. For all her life, she craved a tangible place to pay homage to a mother that she never knew. The site of her death was now the only place to do so. Savoy wanted to bring her here much sooner, but Lola insisted that they wait until they could be assured that some measure of justice was possible. With that now likely, she was ready.

As they walked into the field, they could hear the gentle waves rolling to the shore from the nearby bay. Above them, three osprey chicks were feverishly eating the fresh catch delivered to them by their parents. Their chirps were melodic and desperate. Savoy pointed to the spot near the scattered stones and shells where Maria's body was found all those years ago, and stayed back to allow Lola her space.

Holding the fresh picked daisies she plucked during their walk to the solemn ground, Lola knelt down to place the bouquet on the ground. Until today, she had never known the sad fate of her mother. That *void* was both the cause and effect of her pain. Now, for the first time in her life, Lola had some truth. But it was neither tender nor forgiving. Instead, Lola felt the unshakable pain from believing that her mother was killed because she was born. This overwhelming guilt shook Lola to her core as she broke down sobbing.

Her heart struggled with guilt, even though Lola knew that she was a child then. Unless she could have prevented her own birth, there was nothing she could have done to prevent her mother's death. She also took solace in knowing that the murder of her mother was solved, which in turn, finally freed her spirit forever. With tears in her eyes, Lola looked up at the sky as a gentle breeze blew through the trees above. She reverted to the poetic verse from her favorite movie.

*"Mother is the name for God on the lips and hearts of all children."*

There, in a solitary field in Orient, New York, almost 40 years after the brutal death of her mother, which plunged her life into an unknown abyss, Lola had finally found her God. For the first time in her life, the *void* has been filled, at least somewhat.

Lola looked back at Savoy and reached out her hand gesturing him to come forward.

"I was in church once," she said wiping back tears. "And in his sermon, the priest said 'Only Light will make the darkness dissolve.' This is what you have done Savoy. You shed light on a long forgotten story, and when it shined, those responsible for the darkness could no longer hide. Thank you. Thank you so much!"

Lola leaned over to give him a soft kiss to the cheek.

Savoy was humbled. He did not fancy himself as a hero. He's just a man who followed his heart and instincts to do the right thing. He corrected a wrong that so badly needed correcting, and, in doing so, he became something larger; he became heroic. For the next hour, the two sat in the quiet field thinking about the journey that had brought them, and Maria, together.

# Legacy

After packing up and thanking Laura Wendt for a wonderful stay, we finally began our journey home. I glanced at Lola, who now slept peacefully in the front seat next to me. The breadth of her emotions was unimaginable. A few weeks ago, she knew nothing of her parents, other than that her mother died unexpectedly. She now knows the true story of her mother, who suffered a terrible fate, and of her father, who lived a lie his entire life only to meet the fate he deserved. While this can never replace the gaping hole in her heart, such knowledge undoubtedly will offer at least some amount of comfort to her. As we drove westward past the rolling vineyards, my mind drifted to Maria. Although we've never met, there is no doubt that this quest for justice connected us in ways I never thought possible. Now, her spirit has been set free after being trapped for so long in that lonely field in Orient.

This journey has taught me a valuable lesson, too. In life, you cannot fight against unknown events or things out of your control. All you can do is focus on things within your control to face each chapter head on, without fear, and fully confident in yourself. With that conviction, and a little luck along the way, things will usually turn out fine. On the night of losing my job, I wept as if it was the end of all things good while doubting myself in every capacity. And then I stumbled upon the article of Maria's murder, and several weeks later, those wretched people responsible for her death have been brought to justice. It turns out that my self-doubt was a huge mistake. Instead of some form of rare breed facing extinction, I am a man who cares enough to help others, regardless of how long and how deep my efforts had to go to achieve that goal. If enough people do that, then it will make the world a better place.

We finally left the North Fork and turned onto the Long Island Expressway. I reached over to hold Lola's hand. It was soft and warm, just like her heart. I knew then that I was ready for the next chapter in my life.

# Epilogue

Hoping to receive a lighter sentence, Luther Vale pled guilty to murder and to conspiracy to commit murder and kidnapping. As part of the deal, he also incriminated Winston and Sarah Rivington for their part in the murder-for-hire plot and conspiracy. Unfortunately for Luther, he omitted the tax fraud he committed over the years as the sole proprietor of Acumen Holdings. This deception added more years to his sentence. A despondent Luther Vale attempted to commit suicide in his holding cell while awaiting his sentencing. However, the sheets that he used to fasten a makeshift noose around his neck was no match for the weight of his large frame, as it slipped free, leaving him with nothing more than a bruised throat.

On January 26, 2011, exactly 38 years 4 months and 3 days after he killed Maria Cruz, Luther Vale was finally brought to justice. He stood before the stone-faced federal Judge Clarence Schmidt who sentenced him to 312 months in federal prison. Currently 62 years old, Luther will be eligible for parole at no less than the age of 85.

After the sentence was read and the final gavel fell, a man who sat quietly in the rear of the courtroom inched forward towards the defendant's table.

Before Luther was escorted away, the man yelled, "You killed my dog, you piece of shit. I hope you rot in hell."

With that statement off his chest, Bobby Mandredi left the courtroom peacefully.

Savoy and Lola also sat in the rear of the courtroom on the day of Luther's sentencing. They were compelled to witness the justice against the man who killed her mother, and who caused her life to go into turmoil. After the sentence was handed down, the two hugged each other, and left the courtroom.

Luther had a long way to go before being eligible for parole. He would never reach that day. Just three years into his jail term, Luther Vale was brutally murdered by three gang members after he was overheard making racist remarks against them. With no one to claim his body, he was buried in an unmarked grave near the prison.

§

Seven months after Luther Vale was sentenced to prison, Sarah Rivington appeared in the same federal courtroom to face justice. Contrary to the small audience that appeared at Luther's hearing, Sarah's appearance in court drew a large crowd, all of whom were shocked at the nature of her charges. Much to her dismay, she was at the center of the very scandal she spent her life trying to avoid.

With a frail body and a broken mind, Sarah pleaded not guilty. It was one last effort to defend the Rivington name, which has forever been tainted by the nature of the allegations against her. She was remanded to a modest medical facility in Riverhead, New York to await trial. Just four months later, Sarah suffered a massive stroke, which left her body paralyzed below the neck. For ten days, she had to rely upon a breathing apparatus to keep her alive, until one cold evening on November 17, 2011, Sarah Rivington died in her sleep. She was 75 years old.

§

Although he never played a physical part in, nor was a conspirator to the murder of Maria Cruz, Chet Rivington admitted to his knowledge of the crime, and more importantly, his failure to prevent or report it. He pleaded guilty to criminal complicity to the crime, along with the seven grams of cocaine found in his home, and was sentenced to 84 months in federal prison. With good behavior, he is scheduled to be released in 66 months, when he is 61 years old. In the wake of his conviction, his business collapsed, and much of his properties were seized by the government.

Chet now spends his days alone in prison writing letters to Lola as often as he can. To date, he has written dozens of letters. He was confident in the heartfelt and apologetic words, and hoped that she would visit him, even if just once. One day he received a package in prison from Lola. He scurried back to his cell brimming with anticipation. When he opened the package, he sat in disbelief at what he saw. All of his letters were returned to him unopened. Until that moment, he had not fully comprehended the gravity of the actions taken by him and his family. Now, Chet will spend the remainder of his sentence in prison, and the rest of his life, reflecting on the stinging pain from the realization that his own daughter refuses to recognize his existence.

§

Life was hard for Rosemary Rivington. She was married and divorced three times, and never bore any children. As an heiress of the Rivington family, she anticipated a lucrative inheritance, which was badly needed to feed her addiction to prescription painkillers, and to compensate for her poor business sense, which caused her to lose millions over the years. Rosemary was dismayed to learn that her inheritance will be diminished significantly now that there is another heir to the family, Lola Cruz.

Upon Sarah's death, Rosemary was tasked with arranging the burial for her mother, which was held at a small cemetery on Shelter Island. Other than Rosemary, and Chet escorted by two police officers, no one else attended the funeral.

§

George McBride wrote an op-ed article on the life and death of Maria Cruz. The piece gave him wide acclaim, and the story was picked up by the *New York Tribune* and the *Associated Press*. After all these years, George McBride finally found his scoop! He enjoyed the remaining years of his life living peacefully in the North Fork.

§

Shortly after the conviction of Luther Vale, a press conference was held at the Southold Town Hall by town officials. The room was packed with reporters and concerned citizens. John Conte accompanied Lola and Savoy to the press conference. The three sat in the front row reserved for them. Cameras began to flash wildly and the crowd hushed as Southold Chief of Police Bryce Lattimer entered the room, approached the podium, and issued the following statement.

*"Good morning. In September of 1972, Luther Vale, a former detective of this police department and Trustee of the Town of Southold, was paid by Winston and Sarah Rivington of Shelter Island, to carry out the murder of a young woman named Maria Cruz in nearby Orient, New York. They carried out this heinous act upon discovering that Maria had given birth to a daughter and that the father of the child was their son Chet Rivington.*

*Nearly four decades later, and by the grace of God, this crime has finally been exposed and those who are still alive and responsible shall face the judgment they deserve. Additionally, Mr. Vale will be stripped of all benefits he may have earned during his employ with the Department, and has been immediately dismissed as a town Trustee.*

*The Police department conducted a thorough investigation, and it has been determined that Mr. Vale acted entirely in his own capacity when he murdered Ms. Cruz. He covered up his crimes by manipulating the investigation, which he unfortunately attained control of. There is no evidence that anyone else in the law enforcement community assisted him in any way. We wish to make clear that the Southold Township, it's Police Department, and all the good citizens here and in the surrounding area, completely renounce this brutal act and that we wish to express our sincere condolences to Lola Cruz, the daughter of Maria Cruz, who is here with us today. Now please join us as we offer a long overdue moment of silence for Maria Cruz."*

After a short question and answer session, the press conference ended, and most of those in attendance dispersed. Mr. Lattimer approached Lola and offered her a hug and some words of sympathy.

"Ma'am," he said. "I sincerely regret what happened to your mother long ago and the suffering that you and your family had to endure. I only wish that I could have been here to prevent it."

Lola wiped her tears and thanked him for his kind words. Mr. Lattimer then shook hands with Savoy, before moving toward John Conte to whisper to him.

"I'm glad you got at least one good punch at him, Mr. Conte. I've read the file and that son of a bitch deserved it. You, Officer Conte, are always welcome here."

Beaming with satisfaction, John stood erect as the two men saluted each other before parting ways.

John Conte returned to upstate New York where he could finally enjoy his retirement. He also recently reconnected with Lenny Plev, who resides with his family in Brooklyn, New York. In a teary-eyed moment, both men apologized to each other, and today remain good friends. The following November, John Conte set out into the woods near his home for the opening day of hunting season and on that day, he harvested the second largest whitetail deer in New York State history.

§

The heinous nature of the crimes provided Andre Carter with the federal jurisdiction he needed to prosecute those responsible for them. He built a strong case against each of the defendants, resulting in guilty pleas from Luther and Chet. Although she pled not guilty, Sarah died well before trial. For his exemplary work, Andre Carter was offered an assistant director position in his department. Never one to leave the action that only a criminal prosecutor can enjoy, he respectfully declined the position, and instead opted for a lucrative salary increase. Dre also became an adjunct professor in a law school in New York City, where teaching young minds thrills him almost as much as trial does. Today, Dre is currently spending a much-needed vacation in Aruba.

§

Special Agents Richard Ramos and Andrew Haverstraw are currently on assignment. Their whereabouts are classified information.

§

With all the criminal matters now closed, the Ford truck was returned to its rightful owner, Murray Warshaw. The next day, Savoy and Lola visited Murray and made him a "good offer" to buy the truck from him. Once they took ownership, they paid him to immediately have the vehicle compacted, with its parts melted down to scrap. Murray celebrated his earnings with more than one large bowl of chili and a root beer, which he was finally able to enjoy without interruption.

§

The court ordered paternity test did indeed confirm Chet as Lola's father, therefore making her the beneficiary of the Trust Fund valued at $17.3 million. To avoid any further dealings with the Rivington estate, Lola reached a settlement with their attorneys for an undisclosed, yet very lucrative, amount. Savoy was her representing attorney in the matter. Of all the proceeds Lola received, she kept only a small portion for herself to live comfortably. She donated the remainder of the funds to children's orphanages in New York City and Suffolk County, and made a sizeable donation to the Lower East Side campaign against the proposed gentrification project. She also threw one giant party in a nearby community center for all her neighbors to attend. The posthumous guests of honor were her mother Maria and Lita.

A few weeks later, Savoy and Lola filed a written request with the New York State Department of Corrections, the agency responsible for the operation and maintenance of Potters Field on Hart Island, to search for any records relating to Maria's body. After an agonizing wait, they finally received a response confirming that Maria Cruz was indeed buried in Plot 266-904B on or about June 13, 1973. After the filing of the proper documentation, they were finally granted permission to claim her remains. On January 26, 2010, they held a small ceremony in which Maria's remains were disinterred and buried in the same plot as her mother Lita. Now, when Lola visits, she finally has an adequate place to mourn the death of her mother.

For expenses he incurred during his investigation of the murder of her mother, Lola paid Savoy a modest fee of $1.00. This was an amount far greater than he was willing to accept. Savoy maintains that he got the best gift of all when he asked Lola to marry him a year later and she agreed. The two got married in a small ceremony held at the Oyster Cove Inn in Greenport, where they vacation each year and always bring flowers to the site of her mother's death in Orient. Dre was the best man and John Conte, George McBride, Lucy Fallock, Richard Ramos, and Andrew Haverstraw all attended the wedding hosted by Laura Wendt.

To provide Clubber with a canine companion, Savoy and Lola adopted a Yorkshire terrier named Vito. A big name for a small dog reasoned the couple. The four moved to a modest home on Long Island with a big backyard and even bigger dreams. Now, one year later, the couple is expecting a child. There is a continuous debate between them about what they would name the child if it were a boy. There is no such debate over the name of a girl. She will be named Maria.

The couple outfitted their large garage into an office space for Savoy's burgeoning law practice in which he helps low to middle-income people with a variety of legal needs. That is only half his practice. The other half is dedicated to the "investigative research" of cold cases.

One day, Savoy and Lola were playing in the yard with the dogs, when the phone rang in the office.

"Yes, hold on please," said Lola. "Savoy, it's for you..."

# About the Author

Mark Torres is a husband, father, attorney and now a proud author. As an attorney, Mr. Torres proudly represents thousands of unionized workers in the Greater New York and Tri-State area. *A Stirring in the North Fork* is his debut novel.